Another Time,
Another Place

Another Time, Another Place

a novel by

Mary Verdick

authorHOUSE®

AuthorHouse™
1663 Liberty Drive
Bloomington, IN 47403
www.authorhouse.com
Phone: 1-800-839-8640

Published by AuthorHouse 3/28/2013

ISBN: 978-1-4817-1932-2 (sc)
ISBN: 978-1-4817-1933-9 (hc)
ISBN: 978-1-4817-1931-5 (e)

Library of Congress Control Number: 2013903171

Chapter One

Since she had started her first ballet class at seven Phoebe had thought of nothing but dancing. Like all little girls she yearned to become a prima ballerina someday. But unlike most little girls, even though she went to school, she attended few parties, had very little outside fun. At her own insistence, everything revolved around dance.

She lived, breathed, ate, and thought dance, nothing else, while her parents, Phyllis and Brent Fox, fretted about her. They thought dancing was all very good in its place, but Phoebe was much too intense. Even with excellent grades she had no interest in going to college, an idea her mother pushed all the time. Instead she wanted to go to New York City and study at the School of American Ballet.

Her teacher, Madame Popporov, who had defected from the Soviet Union while on tour with the Kirov Ballet some twenty-five years before, had a real eye for talent and thought Phoebe had an excellent chance. Madame ran the Natasha Popporov School of Dance and Theater Arts in Brookside, Connecticut, and Phoebe had long been her star pupil.

Phoebe was not a great beauty, but her high broad forehead, gray-green eyes, and small straight nose lightly dusted with freckles, was fresh and appealing. Her blond hair, which she usually wore in a bun, was thick and shiny and fell to her shoulders in graceful waves when she let it down. And her shape, for a dancer, left little to be desired. At five-feet-five she weighed 105 pounds and had what was known in ballet circles as a Ballanchine body, after the late great choreographer and founder of the School of American Ballet in New York City. Her neat small head, long neck, slender torso, and well turned-out legs and feet fitted the master's ideal.

Her parents recognized her talent and were proud of her. But they thought it unhealthy for an eighteen-year-old girl, who had just graduated from high school, to have no life but dance. When Phoebe's older sister, Franny, had been home, the phone was constantly ringing and boys were always underfoot, a situation Mrs. Fox considered both normal and desirable. Although as Mr. Fox pointed out, things hadn't turned out for Franny exactly as they'd hope, either.

Nevertheless Mrs. Fox had given Phoebe an ultimatum. She could audition for the New York City School of American Ballet. But if she didn't make it that was it. She was to give up all thoughts of dancing professionally and concentrate on getting into college.

The Foxes were far from poor, but three or four dance lessons a week added up, not to mention the several pairs of toe shoes Phoebe went through in a month at forty or fifty dollars a pair. And even though Franny was on her own now, living in Colorado, the Foxes still had to think of putting Jack and Alex, Phoebe's fourteen-year-old twin brothers, through college.

"So is it a deal?" Mrs. Fox had asked, holding out her hand.

"Deal," Phoebe replied, solemnly shaking.

For the next two months she was happier than she'd ever been as she envisioned herself living and dancing in New York, going to classes, studying with the greats of the ballet world. Maybe she'd even meet Peter Martins himself, the master-in-chief of the New York City Ballet, whom she idolized and whose life-size picture poster dancing in the title role in Ballanchine's Apollo hung in her room.

Madame Popporov, dearest Poppy, was almost as excited as she was. "Fine, ver-ry good!" Poppy beamed as Phoebe executed

2

a perfect adagio movement. "But why so gloomy, my lamb? Must smile, show judges you are having fine time. Do your toes hurt? Am I working you too hard?"

"No-o, never!" Phoebe shook her head. There was a saying in ballet, "Talent is work," and she knew what that meant. If she wanted to really perfect her technique— possibly gain an edge over the thousands of other young dancers, many just as talented and just as dedicated as she—then she could never let up, never lose sight of her goal.

But if the truth were known, lately she was a little tired. Now that school was over she was taking two or three classes a day, six days a week, and her muscles were sore and aching. She had so little energy left, she could barely get out of bed in the morning. At night she was too exhausted to eat. She saw her parents looking at her alarmed and she knew she couldn't keep this pace up for long. But the thought of what lay ahead, the final pay-off, danced before her eyes like some great big shining star. All she had to do was reach out and grab it!

Then came the morning of the audition, August 15, 1992, the most anticipated day of her life. Dressed in a plain black leotard, as the directions had stated, and with her hair tucked securely into a bun so the teachers could see her neck and shoulders, she and her mother were driving to New York, her mother telling her not to be too disappointed if she didn't make it.

"I'll make it."

Mrs. Fox sighed. "I'm sure you will, darling; I don't doubt it for a moment. But it won't be the end of the world if you don't. Remember there're hundeds of girls trying out for this thing, probably all very gifted—and there're only so many places."

"Well, one of them will have my name on it. You'll see, Mom."

At the audition she was first seen with about twenty other students in a class designed to show their proficiency and technique at the barre. These exercises included standard pliés, tendues, and rond de jambs that she had done so often, they were second nature, and she began to lose her nervousness. Even when they moved on to center floor for adagio, pirouettes, and small and large jumps, and one of the other girls deliberately tried to cut her off when she was doing combinations across the floor, she managed to keep her cool, keep smiling, and finished the class in good shape, even managing an especially nice pirouette before the three judges.

Then it was time for her solo variation. She had wanted to do the White Swan variation from *Swan Lake*, but Poppy felt it was too ordinary. "You must do something different to catch their eye; no?"

"Oh, right. Absolutely," Phoebe agreed.

She knew the complete pas de deux from *Le Corsaire*, and she and Poppy also considered La Bayadère from the first act variation from *Giselle*. Finally they settled on a solo from the pas de trios in *Swan Lake's* first act.

It was charming and not too difficult, and she had practiced it so often, she felt she could do it in her sleep. As the first notes of Tchaikovsky floated across the studio, she glanced again at the impassive faces of the three judges, two men and a woman, who also happened to be the ballet mistress of the company, and knew she was as ready as she'd ever be.

And her dancing seemed to bear that out. Whatever else she had done in her dancing career, today's audition surely had to be the best she'd ever performed. She was certain that Poppy had taught her well and nothing was wrong with her technique, the arch of her back, the line of her body, the strength and delicacy of her movements. She had no trouble on pointe, she had a good jump, and most of the time her balance was sensational. So what if her legs felt a little mushy and she was painfully conscious of a blister starting on her right toe.

As the fiery strains of Tchaikovsky continued to flow across the studio, she concentrated on allegro footwork with its many small beats, jumps, and turns, done at an ever increasing rate of motion. Her feet were skimming the floor like a hummingbird's wings and she had the feeling nothing could stop her. The mushiness had left her legs, and in her mind's eye she could almost see Poppy's hand pointing skyward, making minute circles with her index finger, a signal meaning she wanted multiple pirouettes—and as if in answer, Phoebe did fourteen perfect turns on one leg.

Although the ballet mistress didn't change expression, Phoebe sensed the mistress was impressed and she was pleased with herself. Maybe a little too pleased. At any rate, for no reason, two seconds later she messed up a simple pas de bourreé. And then, a split second after that, the unthinkable happened. She fell flat on her fanny, right in front of the judges' table.

Face red and limbs trembling, she scrambled to her feet and picking up the variation on cue, managed to finish it. But the damage had been done!

To calm herself she walked over to the rosin box in the corner and began rubbing her ballet slippers in it. She was aware that the ballet mistress had come up beside her. The woman touched her arm and motioned Phoebe to follow.

At the table the judges said she had a nice dancer's body and that it was obvious she'd worked very hard. She could always teach or dance locally.

"But only a very few dancers become stars, my dear," the ballet mistress said. "It takes an indefinable combination of style, strength, technique, and ambition to succeed in this field."

The ride home was quiet, filled with pain and shattered dreams. Phoebe was so devastated she could barely talk. But the first thing she did when she got home was take Peter Martins' picture off the wall and after wadding it up, throw it in the wastebasket.

In the days that followed she had moments of totally freaking out, when it hurt so much to remember what she'd lost that she didn't want to go on living. Then, completely unexpected, her great-aunt Weezy, who was one of her favorite people, called with what Mrs. Fox dubbed a "wonderful idea". Phoebe didn't think it was so wonderful, but her mother acted as if it was the answer to a prayer.

Her great-aunt Weezy, who'd moved to a retirement residence in Santa Fe, after years of living and working in New York City, wanted to visit her hometown of Denver "One more time," as she put it, to see her older sister Jenna, Phoebe's grandmother. It was a relatively short trip from Santa Fe to Denver, less than four hundred miles, but Weezy couldn't fly because of an inner ear problem. The train seemed to take forever, she said. For the same reason the bus was out of the question.

"But I have this nice little Dodge Dart," Weezy told Mrs. Fox, "and if I drove I could stop along the way if I got tired. Only I don't want to drive alone, it's too boring. So-o I was wondering—do you suppose Phoebe would go with me to share the driving and keep me company, if I sent her a round trip plane ticket from Hartford to Albuquerque?"

"Why, I don't see why not," Mrs. Fox said, and went on to tell Weezy how "delighted" Phoebe would be to accompany her, even though she was the one who was delighted—and why not? After all, it answered the question of, "What to do with Phoebe?" for the next two weeks, which was beginning to be a real problem, since the Foxes wanted to go to Europe for their twenty-eighth wedding anniversary.

When they'd planned the trip back in June, the twins had just gotten jobs as junior counselors at an overnight summer camp, and Phoebe would supposedly be in New York, studying at the School of American Ballet. But when Phoebe flunked her audition it was back to square one. Her parents didn't want to take her to Europe with them. What kind of romantic anniversary trip would that be having a failed ballerina tagging along behind them? But they felt they couldn't leave her alone in her present state of mind. The unexpected trip west would take care of things.

"You'll be helping Aunt Weezy and it'll give you a chance to see Gram again, whom you haven't seen in ages. And not only that," Mrs. Fox hesitated, then continued, her voice elaborately casual, "since you'll be in Denver, you might as well pop by Franny's and see the baby—even if the poor little thing doesn't have a father."

"Franny's baby has a father. The baby's father is just not married to the baby's mother."

"Don't remind me!" Mrs. Fox shuddered. "How that sister of yours, an intelligent girl, could divorce a perfectly marvelous young man—"

"A doctor yet!"

Her mother glared at her. "Don't be impertinent. You know perfectly well what I mean. How your sister, a girl with everything going for her, could leave her nice young husband to take up with that—that cook is just beyond me. And then having a baby with him! Well, it defies all common sense. Not to mention decency. That's why your father and I have washed our hands of Miss Franny. She's made her bed, and now she can lie in it."

Which she seemed to be doing pretty well, Phoebe thought wryly. If Franny were upset by her parents' attitude she gave no indication of it in her emails. Probably because, like Phoebe, Franny knew their mother would relent in time.

In spite of all the bluster, the dire threats about cutting Franny out of their will, both girls knew their mother was dying to hold her first grandchild in her arms. So while she might talk unforgiving it was temporary, proven by the fact that she was encouraging Phoebe to visit Franny and the baby in Denver to bring back a firsthand report.

"I am sort of curious as to what that little girl looks like," Mrs. Fox admitted. "Now if she has Franny's features and is half as light and graceful as you—"

Phoebe wrinkled her nose. "God, Mom, don't wish that on the poor kid!" As for herself, she hoped little Shilo Dawn would keep her feet firmly planted on the ground and have no dreams of Sugar Plum Fairies ever dancing in her head.

Then she'll never be hurt, she thought, squeezing her eyes shut to keep the silly tears from falling.

Chapter Two

The plane was late landing in Albuquerque, causing Phoebe to run through the terminal so fast she got a stitch in her side. Her breath came in short, ragged little gasps and she was convinced she'd never make it outside. But with a last spurt of energy she dashed through the doors—only to see the shuttle for Santa Fe pulling away from the curb.

"Figures," she muttered, dropping her carry-on. Frustrated tears welled up in her eyes. *Oh, cut it out. It's no big deal,* she told herself as she fumbled in her purse for a tissue. She blew her nose. So she'd missed the stupid shuttle. So what? Her great-aunt Weezy had said that if she missed the two o'clock shuttle another would come at three, and she'd meet them both. So there was no need to even call Santa Fe.

She picked up her carry-on and reentering the terminal found a restroom. She went over to one of the sinks against the wall and splashed cold water on her face. Then raising her head she stared intently at her reflection in the mirror. But the reflection staring back at her looked so glum and unhappy she quickly looked away, absentmindedly tucking a strand of hair back into her bun.

After a few minutes, getting ahold of herself, she left the restroom and found her way outside again. Noticing a spot near the curb, which was partially in the shade from an overhang and would give a good view of the arrival of the shuttle, she yanked her purple T-shirt down over her jeans and sat down on her carry-on. But the light was too intense for her eyes, even in the shade it made her head ache, and brought the helpless tears into her eyes again. Closing them she leaned her head back against the building, telling herself she had to stop this senseless crying. It was stupid the way the least little thing could set her off. So she was unhappy not to be dancing anymore? So whose fault was that? Wouldn't the fool shuttle ever come?

Finally when she'd almost given up hope of ever seeing it, the Shuttlejack careened around a corner and came to a stop right in front of her. Picking up her carry-on she climbed aboard, sitting down in the first vacant seat. A pleasant looking man with steel-rimmed spectacles took the seat next to hers and tried to engage her in conversation.

"You live in Santa Fe?"

"No."

"Interested in the art galleries?'

"No," she said again.

Sighing he gave up. She stared out the window. Not that there was much to see. The countryside between Albuquerque and Santa Fe was monotonous, flat, and sparsely covered with grass. They passed sandy stretches and foothills, dotted with juniper and mesquite, now and then clumps of cottonwood, a few scraggly pines. Even though it was only a little over an hour's ride, the journey seemed to take forever. But finally the warm adobe buildings of Santa Fe started coming into view.

Soon they were entering the city proper, by way of the Old Santa Fe Trail. Turning down Alameda, they came to a big, sprawling hotel called the Inn at Loretto. The Inn, which looked like a gussied-up pueblo, was right across the street from Weezy's retirement residence and was the first drop-off point for shuttle passengers. The driver pulled into the courtyard and shut off the engine.

Phoebe picked up her carry-on and started down the aisle, and immediately spied Weezy waiting at the foot of the steps. A woman of medium height with short, curly salt and pepper hair and rosy cheeks beneath eyes of deep, gentian blue, her great-aunt was seventy-years-old. But she was still a looker, Phoebe thought fondly, in her denim skirt and wide Mexican silver belt, a soft white pullover showing off her slender body to perfection.

"Phoebe, darling!" Reaching out, Weezy gathered her great-niece in her arms. "Oh, how marvelous to see you! And what a brick you are to come all this way to help out your poor old auntie."

"Hey, I was glad to come," Phoebe lied. "Anyway it sure beats traipsing all over Europe with Mom and Dad—especially since they didn't want me."

"What? Why, I can't imagine anyone not wanting *you*," Weezy said. Then added with a grin, "But their loss is my gain, as they say. And you know what, honey?" She squeezed Phoebe's hand. "We're just going to have the best old time, you and me."

"I bet," Phoebe said, and she smiled back at her aunt gamely. But inside she was thinking, *Oh, God, how wrong can you be?*

* * *

They left for Denver early the next morning after a simple breakfast of cereal and fruit. As they walked out on the second-story portale opening off Weezy's apartment, the sun came over the Sangre de Christo range, striking a giant spruce at the end of the courtyard and setting it aflame. Next the sun moved on to the pool, turning it deep, iridescent blue, and drove the last of the shadows from the patio, gay with umbrellas and colorful flowers.

"Man, this is one neat place," Phoebe said, impressed, as they made their way along the portale to the elevator. "You'd never guess it was a retirement home, with a med center right next door, you said? It just looks like any nice apartment complex."

"Well, that's the idea," Weezy said, smiling. Reaching her car in the underground garage, they stashed their luggage and got inside. Weezy started the engine, heading for Route 285 through Española. "The management here does pretty well by us old folks," she added.

"You'll never be old," Phoebe said. "But as nice as your place is, I still don't see why you live there. I mean it's not as if you'd broken your hip, like poor Gram, and *had* to live in an assisted-living place, because you couldn't get around too well anymore. You look pretty spry to me."

Weezy smiled again. "Thanks, sweetie. But if the time ever comes when I do need extra help, and it might, I don't want to be a burden on my relatives."

"How could you be a burden? You're family."

Weezy didn't say anything, but reaching over she gave Phoebe's knee a gentle squeeze.

They drove along companionably through the countryside, which was wild and strangely beautiful, switching drivers every fifty miles or so. Before noon they'd made Colorado. They stopped at a little park in Alamosa for the lunch that Weezy had packed in a cooler—roast beef sandwiches, iced tea, and Phoebe's favorite, double-chocolate brownies.

She groaned at the sight of the brownies and from habit shook her head. Then remembering how her situation had changed, she shrugged and said, "Oh, what the heck?" and proceeded to pig out, stuffing one, two, then three of the delicious morsels in her mouth as fast as she could chew them. "I guess since I'm not going to be a dancer anymore, it doesn't matter how fat and gross I get."

"Well, I wouldn't go that far." Laughing, Weezy lifted an eyebrow. Then growing serious, she added, "But what makes you think you can't be a dancer? Just because you didn't ace one audition—"

"One audition!" Phoebe cried. "Oh, Weezy, you don't understand. It wasn't just an ordinary audition. It was *the* audition, don't you see? for the top, the most prestigious ballet school in the country. They take only the best at American Ballet. And if I can't be part of that company, well-ll—"

"You don't want any part of dance? I know that feeling."

"You do?" Surprised, Phoebe stared at her aunt.

"Indeed I do." Weezy nodded, gazing at the purple mountains

in the distance. "When I was your age, just eighteen, I won a scholarship to the Julliard School of Music in New York City. I dreamed of becoming a world-famous pianist, giving concerts, and setting the musical establishment on its ear."

"No kidding." That was news to Phoebe, although she knew her aunt played the piano. There had always been an old upright in the Greenwich Village apartment in New York, where Weezy had lived all those years she was working as associate to Mr. Len Bernard, the big Wall Street financier.

There had also been a piano, another upright, in the vacation cabin Weezy had built in Evergreen, Colorado, where Phoebe and Franny had spent a few weeks each summer growing up. But Weezy had never paid much attention to the piano, as far as Phoebe could tell. On the rare occasions when she did play it was nothing very serious, nonsense ditties when they were smaller, and sometimes Strauss waltzes.

Certainly there'd been no inkling in her behavior that she'd once harbored dreams of becoming a concert pianist. "So what happened?" Phoebe asked. "Wouldn't your folks let you take the scholarship?" She remembered her grandmother saying once that their parents had been strict, conservative.

But Weezy was shaking her head. "Oh, no, I took it. That's how I got to New York. It was during World War Two and my big sister, Jenna, and Wes had an apartment on Perry Street in the Village."

"The same apartment you lived in for so long, where Franny and I used to visit?"

"The same."

"I always liked that apartment," Phoebe said. It was a first-floor through in a brownstone house, with a big, sunny living room and an amazingly compact kitchen with everything in it. There was a good-sized bedroom in back, where Weezy slept, and a smaller bedroom, with a bath between. At the end of the hallway were French doors leading to a perfect gem of a garden.

Phoebe suspected her aunt had stayed there all those years because of that garden. Obviously she didn't have to stay there. "I'm sure if she played her cards right," Phoebe had heard her mother telling her father, "Weezy's boss would find her something more luxurious. All she'd have to do is ask."

"Now, Phyl," Mr. Fox replied mildly, "you don't know."

"I *know*!" Mrs. Fox said. "You don't think for a minute all those trips Weezy takes all around the world with Mr. Bernard are strictly business; do you?"

"I think whatever they are is Weezy's business—and we'd do well to mind our own."

"Oh, you!" Mrs. Fox cried. "You're just like all the others, taken in by those big blue eyes of Weezy's. Well, let me tell you something, my good man. For all her beguiling ways, and I love her to pieces, heaven knows—but still and all Weezy's *not* the sweet innocent she appears. And Bernard's married, don't forget."

"So?"

"So he's never going to divorce his wife to marry Weezy."

And apparently her mother was right, Phoebe thought sadly. "I guess Gram and Gramps didn't think New York was so hot," she said now. "Didn't they return to Denver as soon as the war ended?"

"Yes, but that doesn't mean they didn't like New York. I think they liked it while they were there. Your granddad, being a lawyer, was attached to the adjutant general's office near Times Square, but he also had something to do with Intelligence. I helped Jenna with the housework and the gardening and balancing her checkbook. She wasn't good at numbers." Weezy grinned. "When I wasn't attending classes at Julliard. People were dying overseas in unspeakable numbers, and we knew that, of course, but on the home front life was just so exciting."

"How come?"

"I'm not sure, but everyone pulled together for the war effort. You see, we *believed* in what we were doing so completely. It was a much simpler time. We knew who our enemies were and were prepared to do anything to defeat them. You can't imagine the spirit people had. It was an incredible time to be alive, and New York was sheer magic—so heady and romantic, everything speeded up so."

"Yeah? But what happened to you at Julliard?" Phoebe asked. "Was it as great as you thought it was going to be?"

"Even better," Weezy said, with a smile. "I loved every moment there. My classes, the teachers, the endless hours of practice—all of it was a never-ending joy. I couldn't wait to get there in the morning, and I looked forward to graduation with such hope. But"—sighing she turned her head aside for a moment—"it was not to be. I had to leave Julliard unexpectedly."

"Why? Did you flunk an audition or something?"

"No."

Phoebe thought she saw the glint of tears in her aunt's eyes. "It was nothing that dramatic. I did very well at Julliard. But the war ended. I had to give up my dream."

"Why?" Phoebe asked again. "I mean, if you were doing well—"

Weezy shrugged. "Circumstances changed, that's all. I had to make a living."

"Is that when you went to work for Mr. Bernard?"

"Correct." Weezy nodded. "And I could have done a lot worse, all things considered. But I still remember Julliard, what might have been."

Phoebe heard the echo of sadness in her voice, and reaching over impulsively gave her aunt's arm a little squeeze. "That must have been really rough, turning your back on what you wanted so badly. I'm sorry."

"Why, that's all right, sweetie," Weezy said. "It was all a long time ago. But I wanted you to know I understand how you feel about not making that audition. And I also want you to know that life goes on, in spite of disappointments. As banal as it sounds, it even gets easier after a while."

Maybe for some people, Phoebe thought. *But not for me. Never for me!*

Nevertheless she smiled bravely at her aunt, knowing Weezy only wanted to help.

Chapter Three

When they got back in the car after lunch, it was Phoebe's turn to drive, and Weezy surprised her by saying to take Route 17 at the junction.

"Seventeen?" Phoebe said. "Are you sure? On the map it looks like 285 goes right through to Denver."

"It does, and we'll pick it up again later," Weezy told her. "But 17 is a shortcut. They call it the Shotgun because the road runs in a perfectly straight line for almost sixty miles."

After being on it for a few miles Phoebe could certainly see why the name fit. The road had nary a curve and went through country so flat it was stupefying. Even the towns they passed, Mosca, Hooper, Moffet, did nothing to relieve the monotony, perhaps because they were just wide places in the road containing at most a gas station, maybe a store or two.

Phoebe did her best to stay alert, but after a half-hour of the tedious road her eyelids flickered. She shook her head to clear it and glanced at her aunt, who by now had laid her head back against the seat and was sleeping, or at least dozing Had this boring stretch of country gotten to her, too? Phoebe wondered. Or was it those pills she was always taking on the sly?

Phoebe had noticed her opening the gold pillbox, that she always carried with her, more than once on this trip. Phoebe had seen the pillbox hundreds of times through the years since Weezy used it for everything; stamps, mints, buttons, at one time or another, had all found their way into the pillbox.

As children Phoebe and Franny had loved the pillbox with its flowered cloisonné top in delicate shades of green and blue and gold. In the center of the flowers, lying down, was a white horse with a jeweled horn. The horse was so tiny you couldn't really see it unless you examined the pillbox closely. But it was there.

"Looky, Weezy, looky! Here's a unicorn," Phoebe remembered her five or six-year-old self crying delightedly when she first discovered it. "Here's a pretty little unicorn hiding in the flowers; see?"

"Well, so it is," Weezy said, her blue eyes dancing. "What a smart girl you are to have found it, Phoebe darling." She smiled and hugged Phoebe close. "That's a unicorn all right, and you know what it stands for?"

"What?"

"Paradise—where I resided once."

Phoebe frowned. "How come? In Sunday School they said paradise was heaven."

"Oh, sometimes it's right here on earth."

"Truly?" Phoebe said puzzled. "Then what happens when you die?"

"I think you find it again, if you're lucky," Weezy told her. Then she took the pillbox from Phoebe's hand and held it close against her chest, and there was such a look of longing on her face for a moment it hurt Phoebe inside. And this was the very same pillbox Phoebe had seen her aunt using on this trip for its original purpose—storing pills. She had noticed Weezy popping pills early in the morning, around ten, and again just before they ate lunch.

And the way she took them, so secretively, it was obvious she didn't want Phoebe to see. But Phoebe had seen, and she couldn't help wondering what they were. Pain pills? Tranquilizers? Something more serious maybe? Was it possible Weezy was having health problems? She was seventy, after all, although she didn't look it, and she seemed pretty healthy.

Darn healthy, as a matter of fact. She seemed a whole lot better than Gram. Why even Mom, who was young enough to be her daughter, seemed a little harried at times next to Weezy's unquenchable serenity. Maybe something could be said for the single life, after all. You might miss a bit of fun, but you'd probably escape a lot of frustration, worry, which made Phoebe wonder if her aunt had ever been in love. She wanted to ask her but didn't know how, and as she was debating possible openings, Weezy, bright eyed and refreshed, woke up from her nap.

They continued on their way without any trouble, although outside the little town of Mineral Hot Springs the car sputtered a few times and gave them a scare. But when they stopped for gas the attendant said it was probably just overheated, put water in the radiator and said to take it easy, and they didn't have any more trouble.

A short time later they rejoined Route 285 and found themselves in the mountains again, once more surrounded by beautiful scenery. After the drabness of the Shotgun, the change seemed spectacular, and when Weezy announced it was time she took over, Phoebe happily pulled to the side of the road, and they exchanged places. And it was then that Weezy dropped her bombshell.

"Keep your eyes open for a sign that says Inspiration Peaks Hot Springs Resort. It shouldn't be far now, somewhere around Buena Vista."

"Inspiration Peaks Hot Springs Resort? What's that?"

"The place where we're going to spend the night."

"We're going to spend the night at a resort in Buena Vista?"

"It's not exactly *in* Buena Vista, but somewhere around there I think."

Before she could say anymore they spied a young Hispanic girl, in the orange vest of the road crew, signaling them to stop. Weezy rolled down the window when they came even with her. "What is it, dear?" she asked.

"They're fixing the road up ahead, ma'am, outside of Nathrop," the girl said. "It'll be about a ten-minute wait, I expect."

Actually the wait was closer to half-an-hour. The line of cars behind them stretched out as far as the eye could see before they were given the signal to proceed. And Phoebe wasn't any closer to finding an answer to her question than she'd been in the beginning.

"Why aren't we going straight through to Denver?" she asked. "We must be at least halfway there by now."

"More than half, I'd say. It's only a hundred-and-twenty miles to Denver from the resort, according to the brochure."

"Then why are we stopping?" Phoebe glanced at her watch. "It's only a little after two. We could make Denver by dinnertime—easy."

"Probably. But what's the rush? Inspiration Peaks is supposed to be a very nice place. It's famous for its hot springs. Wouldn't you like to swim, take a soak in natural spring water for a change?"

"I guess," Phoebe said, although the thought had never entered her head.

"Well then keep your eyes open for the sign."

But when they reached Buena Vista, which turned out to be a fair-sized town, they drove up and down the main street for fifteen minutes without seeing any sign advertising the Inspiration Peaks Hot Springs Resort.

"Maybe we ought to stop and ask directions," Phoebe suggested.

"Good idea," Weezy said. "What about that place up ahead?" She gestured with her chin. "Look okay to you?"

"Sure," Phoebe said, glancing at a peeled log building at the end of the street, with a sign over the door saying Roundup Café.

Weezy pulled to a stop before the building, and Phoebe went inside. It was so dim after the bright sunlight she couldn't see much at first, although she made out tables and chairs and a cleared space in back, probably for dancing.

There was a bar along one wall with a couple of customers, and as her eyes became accustomed to the gloom, she saw a man standing behind the bar, polishing glasses. He was middle-aged with sandy hair and small laugh crinkles around his eyes, and he looked pretty friendly.

"Howdy, miss," he said, with a broad smile. "What can we do for you?"

"Hi. I'm looking for the Inspiration Peaks Hot Springs Resort," Phoebe told him. "Do you know where that is?"

Before he could answer, a skinny girl, who looked to be in her mid-twenties, came out of an open door in back. She had whitish blond hair pulled severely back in a ponytail and a long, straight nose that was too prominent for her pinched face. She was wearing skintight jeans and a man's blue work shirt knotted in front, and her skin was so pale, even in the dim light, Phoebe could see the veins underneath. She reminded Phoebe of a scared rabbit the way her eyes, suspicious and wary, jumped about. Yet she came right up to Phoebe and pushing her face up as close as she could, demanded in a quick, edgy voice, "What you aiming to go to Inspiration Peaks for, gal?"

The bartender and the two customers at the bar seemed to find that remark pretty funny. "Maybe she's heard about its hidden assets, Wynonna," one of the customers drawled.

The bartender laughed and added, "Face it, girl, you can't keep every good-looking female you see away from that place, you know."

"Never thought I could, Leroy," the girl snapped. She pronounced it "Lee Roy", with the accent on the first syllable. Then turning back to Phoebe she said sullenly, "You've come a mite too far for Inspiration Peaks. You best go back to Nathrop, the town before, and look for the signs there."

"Oh, darn!" Phoebe said. "They're fixing the road around there, and that'll be another half-hour wait, I bet."

The bartender said, "Well, there's another way. When you get out front make a U-turn, go to the second traffic light and turn left on Rodeo Road. Just keep going on Rodeo up the mountain for about five miles, and you'll run smack into Inspiration Peaks."

"Why, thanks." Phoebe smiled at him. "Is it a pretty nice place?"

"Nah—it's a lousy place," the girl answered for him. "I don't rightly see why a smart-looking tourist like you would want to spend her hard-earned money staying in a dump like Inspiration Peaks."

"Aw, don't listen to her, miss," the bartender said, laughing again. "Our little friend here is a great kidder. Inspiration Peaks is just fine. You'll like it, might even learn to love it. Who knows?"

"Well, thanks again for your help," Phoebe said leaving. "I appreciate it." She returned to the car.

"Did you get directions?" Weezy asked.

"Yep—but you should have seen the strange girl in there. Man, talk about weird! She'd take the prize, hands down."

The bartender's directions were very good though. They had no trouble finding Rodeo Road and drove along for five miles or so. Then climbing a steep grade they made one final turn and spied the resort spread out below them, an attractive group of fieldstone buildings clustered in a valley.

A rushing mountain stream ran through the property, and they could see several outdoor pools, clouds of steam rising from them. A dozen or so people on horseback were coming down a trail through the forest, and even from this distance they looked like they were enjoying themselves. *Might not be such a bad idea spending the night here after all,* Phoebe thought smiling.

Chapter Four

They checked in at the main lodge and were shown to their room. Weezy said she was going to sit out on the balcony and rest a while.

"Oh?" Phoebe looked at her hard. "Are you tired? Don't you feel well?"

"I feel fine," Weezy assured her. "But I'd like to just sit here for a bit, drink in all this gorgeous scenery. Why don't you put on your bathing suit and take a soak, or better yet, a swim? That's what this place is famous for, after all. It would be a real shame to come all this way and then waste it, don't you think?"

"I guess," Phoebe said. A swim might be kind of refreshing. "But I don't want to leave you."

"For goodness sake!" Weezy's mouth twitched with amusement. "You won't be *leaving* me, honey. I'll be right here."

"Well, if you're sure—"

"I'm sure. Now skedaddle!" Weezy pretended to swat her.

"Okay, okay." Laughing, Phoebe put up her hands in mock protection. "No need to get violent."

Still laughing, she opened her bag, pulled out her turquoise bikini, and a few minutes later was walking down the path at the side of the lodge, following the signs saying, Pools. As she came closer she could hear the rushing of a stream, so loud it drowned out any sounds from the highway.

At the charming old bathhouse, over a century old according to a plaque posted on the wall, she undressed and got into her bikini. Then she went out on the deck. There were two pools, neither of them very crowded. She could see the steam rising as she walked over to the nearer one, and after tentatively sticking in a toe she decided to take the plunge and dove in. Her immediate sensation was one of being submerged in a steam cabinet.

She swam up and down the length of the pool, but it was a struggle. In no time she was out of breath. As she was trying to decide whether to stick it out for another few laps or collapse on the deck, she felt a sudden yanking on her big toe. Then a wet head popped up beside her, and a friendly male voice said, "I'm not trying to scare you, but you should take it a little easier in the beginning. The water's a hundred-thirty-five degrees and until folks get a mite used to it, they can find it just a wee bit debilitating."

"Now you tell me!" Phoebe groaned and sank in a mock faint, her head slipping beneath the water.

"Hey!" Her would-be rescuer caught her beneath the armpits and pulled her up beside him. "Don't pass out on me, girl. You all right?"

"Sure," Phoebe said. "Fine." Feeling a little flustered, however, she broke away from him, although it was oddly pleasant being held in his arms. She pulled herself up on the side of the pool and slid onto the deck in a split.

"You the lifeguard?"

He grinned and got out of the pool, too. "I work at the resort, do a bunch of things around here."

"Like what, for instance?"

"Oh, keep an eye out for tourists like you, to make sure they don't hurt themselves."

"Funny—you're the second person in half an hour to call me a tourist. How do you know I'm not a native?"

"With those legs? I would have remembered. Hotdamn!" He shook his head. "I swear you're the only person I ever saw whose legs are twice as long as the rest of her. Are you a model?"

"Nope," Phoebe said. She took the towel he offered and slung it about her shoulders. No one had ever mistaken her for a model before, and it secretly pleased her—especially since the young man standing before her was attractive enough to be a model himself. Tall and deeply tanned, he had a full, sensuous mouth and prominent cheekbones setting off a finely chiseled face.

His hair, light and wavy, was already beginning to dry in the bright mountain sun, and when he smiled, which he was doing now, a dimple danced in his cheek.

"If you're not a model," he was saying, "I figure you're a contortionist then."

"A contortionist?" That really made her giggle. "Where do you get such ideas?"

"Well-ll, that's a pretty nifty looking split you're doing there. Not everyone's that limber is all I meant."

"This? It's child's play," she said, bringing her knees up to her chest and hugging them. "Actually I studied to be a dancer for years. Splits were par for the course."

"Is that a fact? And where might that be that you did all this studying?"

"Brookside, Connecticut. It's a suburb of Hartford."

"Connecticut? Gosh! That's a right far piece from here. You ever been in Colorado before?"

"Lots of times—although never in this part of the state. My grandmother lives in Denver, and my mother grew up there."

"You don't say. What's your name, by the way?"

"Phoebe Fox."

"Phoebe? Cody Moon," he said. "Tell me, was your mom an admirer of J. D. Salinger, by any chance?"

Phoebe laughed. "How'd you guess? My mom met my dad in college in an English lit class when they both wrote a paper on *Catcher in the Rye*. She got an *A*-plus and he got an *A*-minus, but it was the start of a beautiful friendship."

He grinned. "I can imagine. I must have read *Catcher* half-a-dozen times myself. I really dug Holden and his feelings for his little sister Phoebe."

"Oh, so did my mom," Phoebe said, pleasantly surprised that this guy was not only good looking but literate. "Actually Mom adored Salinger's whole Glass family, too, and all the stories he wrote about them. I have an older sister named Franny, and when my twin brothers were born, Mom seriously thought of naming them Zooey and Seymour, if you can believe it. But Dad put his foot down, saying enough was enough, and named them Alex and Jack."

He laughed. "Which I'm sure they'll thank him for. By the way, what college were your folks going to when they hooked up with Mr. Salinger?"

"The University of Colorado in Boulder."

"C. U.? You don't say. I hear that's a pretty good school. I won a scholarship for there when I graduated from high school in June."

"No kidding. You must be pretty smart."

"Nah." He looked embarrassed. "I was valedictorian—but there were only thirteen in the class. C. U. gives all the valedictorians in the state a scholarship every year. It's automatic."

"Still, that's quite an honor. I might be going there myself someday," she told him, although until that very moment she'd never considered it. Of course C. U. wasn't the School of American Ballet in New York City, but still— "What are you going to major in?"

"Engineering—if I go."

"If? Is there some question about it?"

"Ah, I don't know. I quit school for a couple of years to earn some money, so I'd be older than most of the kids in the freshman class."

"I don't think that would make any difference."

"Well, we'll see." Shrugging he extended a hand. "Want to go down to the creek and sit on the rocks for a while?"

"I wouldn't mind," she said, and she took his hand and easily rose to her feet.

They went down a few steps to the creek, sat on smooth, flat stones, and dangled their feet in the water. Steam from the underground springs rose all around them, giving the scene a misty, surrealistic quality. He told her there were twenty hot springs which supplied odorless, crystal-clear water for the resort's bathing facilities.

"And to think I never heard of this place," Phoebe marveled, shaking her head.

"Oh, well," he said grinning, "that's not surprising. Inspiration Peaks is one of Colorado's best-kept secrets. Our pools are all spring fed, and there are also private indoor hot tubs at the bathhouse."

"My aunt would like that, I bet."

"You traveling with your aunt?"

"That's right. She's my great-aunt, actually."

"How long you gonna be here, Phoebe?"

"Just for tonight."

"Just one night?" He looked disappointed. Then brightening he added, "But one night's better than nothing, I reckon. Say, how'd you like to go into Buena Vista after I get off work, and take in a movie?"

"I'll have to check with my aunt first, but that sounds like fun."

"Great!" His grin lit up his face. "Then I'll see you at dinner; okay? I've got to run now and get the dining room ready for the thundering herd." And so saying he gave her hand a little squeeze and took off, his long legs disappearing into the mist.

Phoebe sat there for several minutes, a bemused smile on her face, wondering if the encounter had really happened. It had been so unexpected, so strange, and at the same time so exciting, the whole thing was something like a dream.

In the bathhouse she shed her bikini, and before she hopped in the shower she took a hard, critical look at the body in the mirror, as she'd done dozens of times through the years. But this time instead of wondering if it was a dancer's body, her face suddenly hot, she wondered if it was a body to attract a man. Her legs were long and shapely, as he'd noticed, her breasts not too large but high and firm, her small waist flowed easily into gently rounded hips—and not a muscle bulged anywhere. It wasn't too bad, she decided, all things considered. And maybe tonight she'd let her hair out of the bun, let it flow, and see what happened. The possibilities excited her.

When she got back to the room she noticed Weezy had changed from her denim skirt and sweater into a white silk shirt with long, flowing sleeves and black palazzo pants with a satin stripe down the side.

"Wow!" Phoebe said. "Get you! What's the occasion?"

"No occasion." Weezy smiled. "I just felt like getting a little spruced up. After all it's not every day I'm honored with the company of my beautiful great-niece."

Phoebe felt her face turning scarlet. She was incredibly pleased by the compliment, although honesty made her say, "Ah, Weezy, I'm not beautiful. Franny's the knockout in the family, remember?"

"You're both knockouts for my money. Besides you should see how your eyes are sparkling, darling. Did something special happen to you this afternoon?"

"Well—ll, I did meet this really nice guy at the pool. He's way cute—and not only that, he's smart, too."

"Sounds promising. Tell me more."

"There isn't much to tell. He works here at the resort, so you'll probably see him tonight in the dining room. He's won a scholarship to Boulder. And he asked me to go to the movies tonight in Buena Vista. I said yes—if that's all right with you," she added quickly.

"Well, I don't see why not. Just as long as you don't stay out too late. I'd like to leave for Denver pretty early tomorrow."

"Oh, I know. I won't be late. I just wish I knew what to wear."

As she talked she started rummaging through her carry-on, not that there was much to choose from. She had brought several pairs of jeans and tops, but only one dress, a sheath in black and white polka dots, with a swishy hem that fluttered with every step she took. She remembered Poppy saying once, when seeing her in it, that the dress "performed well" and it had long been one of her favorites. But thinking of Poppy brought back memories of her failed career.

Even though she'd vowed every day not to think of it, she hadn't been able to keep from reviewing that ghastly audition over and over in her mind. But tonight things would be different, she told herself as she pulled the dress over her head. Tonight she'd just concentrate on having a good time. Imagining life without continual practice and aching toes shouldn't be hard.

Then she glanced at her aunt and wondered what was wrong. In the last few seconds Weezy's face had turned almost chalky, and she was staring at Phoebe in the oddest way.

"What is it?" Phoebe asked, a little frightened.

"That dress." Weezy's voice trembled. "Those black and white dots. I had a dress like that during the war, over fifty years ago. Of course the style was different—my dress was a shirtwaist with little puff sleeves and a very full skirt, but the black and white polka dots were just as gay as yours."

Phoebe smiled. "Did you have a good time in your dress?"

"Did I? Ah, darling." Impulsively she caught Phoebe's hand and pulled her down beside her on the bed. "The first time I wore my dress was in the apartment on Perry Street in New York. Jenna had bought it for me as a going-away present."

"Where were you going?"

"I wasn't. But your grandfather Wes, Jenna's husband, had been transferred to Washington, D. C. on temporary duty for a couple of months, something very secretive with the War Department, and Jenna was dying to go with him. Jenna was sweet and kind of scatterbrained, but she had a strong sense of duty and didn't feel right about leaving her baby sister alone. I remember one morning when we were breakfasting in the garden and Jenna told me that she'd promised our folks, on word of honor, to look after me.

"And you *have*, a hundred percent," Weezy told Phoebe she'd assured her. "Then I told her I was perfectly capable of taking care of myself."

"I'm sure you are," Jenna had said. And this is the conversation that took place between Jenna and her a few minutes later, Weezy told Phoebe.

"Maybe a change of scenery for a few months would be good for Wes and me," Jenna said. "Who knows? I might even get pregnant."

"You'll get pregnant," Weezy said, knowing how desperately her sister wanted a baby. "Didn't the doctor say sometimes those things take time?"

"Sure, but what does he know?" Jenna said, suddenly jumping to her feet, her pretty face a picture in despair. "We try and try, but nothing happens, and we've got so much to offer a kid, at least I think so. If you ask me it's damn unfair!" She started pacing up and down, then abruptly stopped before a rather pathetic looking little rose bush, that was drooping at a really listless angle. "Heck, I can't even grow roses anymore," she said, plucking a leaf from the bush and crushing it between her fingers. "I tell you I must be cursed."

"Oh, Jenna, come on," Weezy said, smiling at her sister. "You're exaggerating."

"No, I'm not. It's absolutely true!" Jenna insisted, her normally gay insouciance completely deserting her. "Remember what that woman in the garden shop, where I bought the bush, told me? She said the silly thing was guaranteed to bloom. And I've done everything right—watered it, bought special feed, fertilizers, the whole kit and caboodle, but you see any roses? Of course not!" Her voice broke miserably. "The poor thing's dying. You know it is."

"Well, so what? It's no great loss," Weezy said. "Look, maybe you should stop worrying about getting pregnant for a while and just go to Washington with Wes and have fun. See the sights, go to the embassy parties, concentrate on having a good time, relax—and who knows what might happen?"

"You're right," Jenna said. "What have I got to lose?" And shaking her shoulders, suddenly smiling, she took Weezy shopping that afternoon and bought her a pretty new dress. Then a few days later she left for the capitol with her husband, after Weezy assured her again she'd be just fine, and practically pushed her out the door.

Chapter Five

"But I did feel a little lonely," she admitted to Phoebe now. "After all I'd never been completely on my own before, and if truth were told it was kinda scary, all by myself in that big city."

"So what did you do?" Phoebe asked.

"The obvious," Weezy said. "Combed my hair, put on fresh lipstick, and got into my pretty new dress. Then I sat down at the piano and started playing Strauss' *Voices of Spring* because it was the gayest, larkiest song I could think of."

"Did it work?"

"Like a charm. Right in the middle of it, though, I had the distinct impression that someone had come into the garden and was watching me. Strangely enough, it didn't make me nervous. I finished the piece and glancing out the French doors saw a young soldier sitting on the bench beneath the copper beech tree."

When the soldier realized she'd seen him he smiled and started clapping. "Bravo!" he cried. "Do you know *Artist's Life* by any chance?"

"Of course," Weezy said, and she turned back to the keyboard and played it through flawlessly, then finished with a rousing rendition of the *Blue Danube.*

"That was delightful," the soldier said. "Really superb. You have a transcendental technique, if I may be so bold as to say so."

Weezy laughed. "A what?"

"A transcendental technique."

"You don't say." She thought he was probably pulling her leg, but something made her ask, "Are you a critic, by any chance?"

"Nope," he said, looking amused. "Nothing that grand. But my mom teaches piano, composition, at a college near home, and I've picked up some of the jargon. By osmosis, I guess."

"And where might home be?"

"Junction City, Kansas."

"No kidding," Weezy said. And then she told him she was from Denver, and he said they were practically neighbors, two Westerners like that. And with that he jumped to his feet, and she saw he was tall and lanky, and his uniform didn't fit very well. But he had the most remarkable eyes, bright and luminous, full of mischief and fun—and something else.

"You sure are one fine pianist," he said. "And I bet you have other talents, too. So, I was wondering, could we pursue those?" He took a tentative step forward.

"Wait a minute, soldier. Not so fast," Weezy said. "How'd you get in the garden anyway? I thought the gate was locked."

"Oh, I didn't come through the gate. I came down the stairs. The agent said the apartments share the garden. But if my presence disturbs you—"

"No-o," she said, and shook her head, "it's not that. It's just that no one's been in the upstairs apartment since I've been here— although we heard the government had bought the property."

"Who's 'we'?"

"My sister and her husband. This is their apartment. But they've gone to Washington for a couple of months. My brother-in-law's on temporary duty with the adjutant general's office here."

"Well, isn't that interesting? I'm on temporary duty myself, while I take a course at New York University."

"Really?" she said. "Would that course have anything to do with Intelligence?"

He looked startled for a moment. "What makes you think that?"

"I'm not stupid," she said. "I know my brother-in-law is into something very hush-hush, and since you're living in this government apartment, well, it stands to reason—"

"Hey, you're not only a good pianist, you're pretty smart too. What's your name, by the way?"

"Weezy," she told him. "Weezy Burton."

"Weezy?" He scratched his brow. "Don't think I've ever heard that name before."

"It's a nickname. My real name is Louisa, but when I was two, or so the story goes, I couldn't pronounce Louisa and it came out Weezy, which stuck. No one's ever called me anything else."

He smiled. "Well, it's mighty cute. Different, too."

"I guess," Weezy said. Were his eyes, with those incredibly long lashes, blue or green? She couldn't tell for sure, but she was certain they were the most beautiful eyes she'd ever seen. And that smile! Irresistible! It seemed to come from somewhere deep inside him and lit up his whole face. "So what do they call you?" she asked, wondering why her mouth felt so dry.

"Mickey," he said. "Mickey McGuire. Mickey's a nickname too. My real name is Reinhard."

"Reinhard? Golly! I'm *certain* I've never heard that name before."

"Probably not. It's German. My mother's from Germany. She came to New York when she was eighteen to study at Julliard. She'd won a scholarship there."

Weezy stared at him amazed. "What a coincidence. That's where I study."

"Julliard? I'm not surprised. You play so beautifully."

"Oh, I don't know about that. But thanks."

"You're more than welcome." He smiled. "But say—" he scratched his forehead again, "—I just had an idea. Would you take pity on a poor lonesome soldier and ask me in? We could discuss music, or whatever—"

31

Weezy's voice trailed off....

"**But** what happened?" Phoebe prompted. "Did you ask him in—or what?"

"Of course," Weezy said. "I not only asked him in, I invited him to dinner. It seemed the patriotic thing to do."

"Natch." Phoebe giggled.

Actually, Weezy added, he'd invited her out to dinner, but she'd noticed there were no stripes on his sleeve, which meant he was just a private. And she knew privates didn't make much money. So she said, casually, and to her own surprise, "Say, why don't we stay here and I'll whip up something."

Of course there wasn't any meat in the fridge. It was wartime, and she'd used up all her ration stamps. But she made her mother's delicious cheese strada and a big salad, and for dessert she served the lovely plump strawberries that she'd found just that afternoon in the little market on the corner. And he raved about the meal and had two helpings of everything.

"I swear that's one of the best meals I've ever had," he told her. "You're absolutely amazing."

"Oh, sure." She laughed. "Marvelous! Look, just because I can sort of throw a meal together doesn't mean anything."

"Throw a meal together nothing," he said. "Nope, not only are you a great cook and can play the piano like a professional, but you're a real pleasure to look at, too."

"Ah, go on with you," she said embarrassed. But she could feel little tickles of excitement racing up and down her spine, and when he caught her hand and maneuvered her down beside him on the couch, she didn't resist. Instead she reached in her pocket and found a package of Camels she'd been hoarding, and lit a cigarette for him. And when he asked her what she did for excitement she told him she didn't do much except practice the piano. "You know that old joke about how you get to Carnegie Hall? Well, that's my life, more or less. Practice, practice, practice."

"But don't you have any hobbies? Fun things to do on the side?"

She shook her head. "There isn't time. I haven't been to the movies in ages, and I used to love to figure skate—but no more."

"Figure skate? How interesting. Were you good at it?"

"I wasn't bad," she confessed. "I actually won a figure-skating competition once at Evergreen Lake, outside of Denver, when I was twelve. I got a medal and fifty dollars as a prize, and I was on top of the world, let me tell you. But I had to give it up because it took too much time away from the piano. So now I just skate occasionally, when I can work it in, you know? So that's my story. What about you?"

"What about me? Well, let's see now." He pulled on his chin, as if considering. "I went to Columbia, my father's alma mater, and majored in History, which was a big disappointment to Dad. He's an engineer, a very good one, too, and he wanted me to follow in his footsteps. But I always wanted to teach."

"On the college level?"

"Nope, nothing that grand."

"High school?"

He shook his head. "Not that either. It might sound strange to you—it does to most folks—but I want to work with little kids, five- or six-year-olds, after the war. I know the pay's lousy and a grade-school teacher's job is not prestigious, but think of the vast opportunity for molding little minds. I believe if you start kids off right, with a good foundation, they'll have a better than average chance of growing up strong and becoming decent, law-abiding citizens. But—" he suddenly flushed, "—don't get me started on that. A lot of people think it's a crazy idea."

"Then they're the crazy ones," Weezy said. "I think it's a wonderful idea, very brave and inspiring. And—" she hesitated, searching for just the right word and finding it finally. "Prophetic!" she announced triumphantly.

"Really? You really mean that?" he seemed clearly surprised at her reaction. "Tell me, how'd you get to be so sweet?"

"I don't know," she said, swallowing, the tenderness in his eyes

33

leaving her feeling weak and vulnerable. "Maybe I had to be to attract an extra-special guy like you."

*   *   *

"What a neat story," Phoebe said, when Weezy paused, her face aglow. "Did you ever see Mickey again?"

"Oh, yes, quite a few times," Weezy said. Lifting a hand she brushed a strand of hair from her face. "He was living right upstairs so I saw him often until he finished his course at NYU. Then he had to leave. But I've always remembered that black and white polka dot dress and what a good time I had in it. But what am I doing, rambling on like this?" Giving her shoulders a little shake, she let go of Phoebe's hand and got up from the bed. "I'm sure I never looked as pretty in my dress as you look in yours, sweetie. So—shall we go into dinner?"

"Sounds good to me," Phoebe said. "I'm starved." And she thought of how nice it was going to be for a change not to have to worry about every single morsel she consumed. But she also thought how strange it was that her great-aunt Weezy could recall so vividly a chance encounter with a young man that had taken place over fifty years before. He must have been one cool guy, that Mickey McGuire, and she hoped she'd learn more about him.

Chapter Six

*C*ody came right up to them in the dining room, as if he'd been waiting just for them. He was tall, even taller than she'd thought that afternoon, and lean, in a lithe, sinewy way. He was wearing a white button-down shirt, open at the neck, with the sleeves rolled up, and freshly laundered jeans tucked into a pair of great-looking cowboy boots. To Phoebe the effect was breathtaking.

She introduced him to her aunt, and as he filled their water goblets, she could tell Weezy was impressed. "Where'd you say you picked him up?" she asked after Cody had taken their orders.

Phoebe laughed. "Believe it or not, it was the other way around. He did the 'pickin', although I must admit I was more than willing. As I said, it happened at the pool. He just started talking, and he seemed okay. He's going to C. U. in the fall."

"Hmm-mm. Well, if he's an example, you have excellent taste in men, sweetie."

"Thanks," Phoebe said blushing, wondering if her aunt had any idea just how little experience she'd really had with men. She decided not to enlighten her, however, and feeling quite worldly and sophisticated concentrated on her excellent dinner.

Cody was supposed to work 'til nine, but since it wasn't a busy night in the dining room he got one of the other waiters to cover for him. He and Phoebe left the lodge at eight-thirty. They went out to his pickup, a red Chevy that had seen better days, and were soon barreling up the mountain.

He went so fast Phoebe had to hang on to the seat to keep from falling against him, but they made the movie in time, not that it would have mattered much if they hadn't. A science-fiction flick, the movie was so awful it was funny.

"Have some popcorn?" Cody asked, holding out the enormous tub he'd bought in the lobby.

"Thanks. I wouldn't mind," Phoebe said. She took a handful, then another. The popcorn was delicious. Maybe it was the crisp mountain air that made it taste so good, she told herself, before she realized the air in this packed little theater was anything but crisp. It smelled more like an old sock, or a ballet studio after a practice session. The thought plunged her into sadness momentarily. But she soon got over it.

"How 'bout if I get us some soda to wash down the popcorn?" Cody asked.

"No, thanks. I'm fine," she said, realizing with a start that she meant it. If she wasn't exactly bubbling with joy, she was filled with a newfound peace and contentment that she hadn't felt since she couldn't remember when. Tonight no past shadows were haunting her, and for a change, she felt really happy and alive. And she couldn't help wondering if the handsome young man sitting beside her had anything to do with this new state of well-being. At any rate she was enjoying the warm glow pulsing through her, giving her new confidence, and she relaxed even when he put his arm around her.

The stars were so close, when they came outside, she had the feeling she could reach right up and touch them, and his arm was still loped companionably about her shoulders. When they reached the pickup, he glanced at the lighted dial of his watch, then at her. "Kind of early," he said, "only a little after ten. How'd you like to go some place and dance, seeing as how you're all dolled up in such a pretty dress?"

She smiled and refrained from saying, "This old thing?" although it was on the tip of her tongue. "Fine. Anything you want to do is fine with me, Cody."

"Anything?" he teased, and reaching out gave a playful tug on her hair, which hung loose and flowing to her shoulders. "Hotdamn, if you aren't something!"

"Ah, go on," she said, wondering if he could tell she was blushing.

He helped her into the pickup, started the engine, and to her amazement drove straight to the Roundup Café. "Hey, I know this place," she said surprised. "My aunt and I stopped here today to get directions to Inspiration Peaks."

"Yeah? Friend of mine works here," Cody said. "Like you two to get acquainted—if that's all right with you."

"Sure," Phoebe said. She wondered if the friend he was referring to could be the bartender, which wouldn't have surprised her. As she remembered, he'd been very nice. What did surprise her was the Roundup, which seemed like an entirely different place at night than in the daytime. It was so packed with people, it was jumping. A blast of country music hit them as Cody pushed his way inside, but he cleared a path through the crowd with his shoulders and finally found them a vacant spot near the bar.

"Where's that waitress?" he demanded, pretending to bang on the table. "What does a guy have to do to get a little service around here?"

"Hold your horses, Buster," a vaguely familiar voice said.

Phoebe looked up and almost fell off her chair as she realized, with a start, that it was the same kooky girl she'd run into that afternoon when she came in here to ask directions to Inspiration Peaks. She didn't know why, but the sight of the girl struck her as vaguely threatening.

The girl had exchanged her jeans for a fringed buckskin skirt and a fancy Western shirt embroidered with flowers, but she was still painfully plain. Until she smiled, when the pinched face lit up, expanded, was transformed, as she gazed adoringly at Cody.

She came right up to them and throwing her arms around his

neck hugged him hard. Embarrassed, Phoebe turned her head aside. After a moment Cody pulled away from the girl and reaching for Phoebe's hand introduced them. "Wynonna, this is a new friend of mine, Phoebe Fox. My sister Wynonna, Phoebe."

His sister! Well! "Hi," Phoebe said, letting out her breath, which she hadn't been aware she was holding until just that moment.

"Howdy." Wynonna nodded, and studied Phoebe's face as intently as though she were reading a road map. "Say, haven't I seen you someplace before?"

"Yes, this afternoon. I stopped in here to ask directions to Inspiration Peaks," Phoebe said.

"Oh, yeah, I remember now. Well-ll—" the thin lips curved in a smirk— "congratulations. I see you didn't waste any time once you got there."

"What do you mean?"

"I mean it's downright awesome the way you little gals from the East come out here and latch on to my poor, innocent baby brother, before he rightly knows what hit him most of the time."

"Now, Sis, let's not get personal," Cody said. Grinning, he turned to Phoebe. "How 'bout a drink? What's your pleasure?"

"A diet Coke would be fine."

"Make that two, Wynonna."

His sister frowned. "You don't need no diet Coke, sonny-boy. You're too skinny as it is. How 'bout if I bring you a regular Coke, and a nice bowl of nachos with jalepeño?"

Cody sighed. "Now, Wynonna, who appointed you boss?"

"*I* appointed me boss," she snapped, "because I know what's best for you."

"Sure, Sarge, whatever you say." He scowled fiercely at his sister for a moment, then closing one eye in a wink, started to laugh. Soon Wynonna was laughing with him.

It was amazing, Phoebe thought, when you studied their two faces, how much alike they were. Yet Wynonna was plain, almost homely, while Cody, with more or less the same features, except they were arranged a little differently, looked nothing short of fantastic. It seemed unfair.

"You mustn't mind Wynonna if she comes across a little strong at times," Cody was saying after his sister left to get their order. "She raised me since I was a pup, and she thinks that gives her certain privileges—even if I don't always agree."

"Where were your parents?" Phoebe asked curious.

"They left."

"Both of them?"

"Yep." He nodded. "Our daddy disappeared when I was nine, just walked off. Mama did her best, but it was just too much trying to bring up two kids alone with little money. So the day after my tenth birthday she took off, too. The last we knew she was somewhere on the West Coast. She used to send us a postcard now and then, but we haven't heard from either one of them in years."

"Gosh!" Phoebe was shocked. "What did you guys do?"

"Well, Wynonna and I made a pact to stick together, that was the first thing, the important thing. Then she quit school and got a job. She was only fifteen, but she lied about her age. I worked, too—summers and after school."

"Where did you live?"

"Oh, we have this mobile home our mama left us. It's in a trailer park in Nathrop, the little town before here, and it's not very fancy. But it's all paid for, free and clear. We just have to pay a monthly rent for the space, which isn't much, and a little for heat and light—so we manage. Actually Wynonna's seen to it that we've always managed pretty well." He spoke lightly, but Phoebe heard the pride in his voice when he mentioned his sister.

So that was why the girl was so bossy, so possessive. She thought she owned him because she'd brought him up. But she was still just his sister, Phoebe told herself.

Wynonna came back just then with their drinks and a huge bowl of cheese-covered nachos. Phoebe shifted uncomfortably under that hot, unwavering gaze. She felt that with a little encouragement,

Wynonna would hang around all evening, guarding her property. Fortunately they were so busy in the bar she couldn't linger.

The bartender hollered at her, and muttering under her breath she turned to leave. But not before telling Cody to stick around, saying she might want a ride home. "My old dogs are killing me and I aim to leave early, if I can. Understand?"

"Gotcha," Cody nodded.

Wynonna left, and Cody turned to Phoebe again, who'd listened to this conversation with growing uneasiness. "Your sister's going home with us?"

"Course not." He grinned. "It's just a joke. Leroy, the bartender, will take her home, as always. Leroy owns the joint, and he's crazy about Wynonna. Wants to marry her."

"Does she want to marry him?"

"Can't say. She thinks he's okay, but he's quite a bit older, and Wynonna says we don't need anyone else. She says we do all right, just the two of us."

"What's she going to do when you go away to college?"

"Oh, well . . . " He shrugged and looked uncomfortable of a sudden. "That's still a ways off. Come on, let's dance."

He stood up and held out his hand. Their fingers touched and a tingle went up her spine. Then she noticed Wynonna across the room. No matter where she was those hot, unblinking eyes followed Cody constantly as she moved about, taking peoples' orders, setting food and drinks down before them. It was unnerving, but Phoebe decided it wasn't going to bother her.

They went out on the crowded dance floor and Cody staked out a place for them and introduced her to the two step and the traveling cha cha. He was circumspect, easy going, at first. But when the three-piece band went into a waltz, he pulled her closer. Now she could feel his legs against hers, feel their stomachs touching, and strange thoughts invaded her mind. Like—how would he look without clothes, how would his naked body feel next to hers? The thoughts made her blush, and she buried her burning face in his shoulder. But that didn't help. She felt dizzy with the smell of him, so warm and clean and male. She could feel the muscles of his shoulders moving beneath her hand, and her stomach tightened.

She wanted this to go on forever, it was so wonderful. Yet the intensity of it scared her, too. Such emotions were all so new, they were overwhelming. So while she hated it to end, at the same time it was almost a relief when the music stopped and they went back to the table.

They sipped their drinks and polished off the last of the nachos when suddenly Cody said, "Whatta you say we ditch this joint?"

She was a little surprised but quickly responded, "Okay by me."

"Great. Then let's go." He threw some bills on the table, then catching her hand, pulled her down beside him on the floor.

"Keep it low," he whispered. When she tried to straighten up he put his hand on her head and pushed it gently down again. They crawled out of the Roundup practically on their hands and knees.

Phoebe was giggling so hard she was almost in tears by the time they got outside. "I can't believe we really did that!" she gasped.

Cody's eyes shone with excitement. "Saves a lot of explaining." Hand-in-hand they ran to his pickup and got inside. "Now where, pretty girl?"

"You tell me." Her voice sounded strange, not like her voice at all. She wrapped both arms around her knees and waited.

"Well, now don't know how this'll sit with you—" he put both hands on the steering wheel, started beating a little tattoo with his fingers. "But I've got a suggestion. What would you say . . ." he turned and looked at her, and she felt something jump inside her. "What would you think about going to my trailer and having another dance? At least it won't be crowded, and you don't have to worry about Wynonna. She won't be off for hours."

But it wasn't his sister she was worried about. What would happen if she went to his trailer, and they started dancing, holding each other close? The possibilities were so dazzling, so terrifying, she hardly dared think of them.

But before she got completely carried away, she reminded

herself that she hardly knew this boy. He was different, unique, a wonderful human being she was sure. She felt that in every fiber of her being. But she and Weezy were leaving for Denver tomorrow, and she might never see him again.

Nervously she ran her tongue over her dry lips. She'd never known her lips to be so dry, while strangely the palms of her hands were soaking wet. After a moment she heard herself saying slowly, reluctantly, "I don't think so, Cody—much as I'd like to. I promised my aunt I wouldn't stay out late, and it must be almost eleven. She'll be wondering what in the world's happened to me."

If he'd coaxed a little she might have changed her mind. But he immediately snapped to attention. "Oh, right. You gotta go. I understand. I'll take you back to the lodge right away. No problem."

It doesn't have to be right away, she cried inside. *At least not right this second.*

She was hoping he'd stop somewhere along the road so they could talk, exchange addresses, phone numbers maybe. But he suddenly seemed in an incredible rush to get her back.

They were barreling down the road, going so fast Phoebe felt sure some of her teeth had shaken loose, when he pulled to a stop before the lodge. "Well, here we are, home sweet home," he said, with a screech of brakes. Then he jumped out of the pickup and dashed around to her side to open the door. "So long, Phoebe. Nice meeting you. Good luck."

"Same here, Cody. And thanks—thanks for everything. I had a good time."

"Glad you enjoyed it," he said. Then giving a jaunty little salute with two fingers, he got back in the pickup and gunned off.

Well, kid, you really blew that one, she told herself. Watching his taillight disappearing in the distance, she sensed that she'd hurt his feelings, although she hadn't meant to. That had been the furthest thing from her mind, and now thanks to her own stupidity, her cowardice, she'd never see him again. A sob rose in her throat and almost choked her. But stoically she went to the room, unlocked the door, and since Weezy was obviously asleep, undressed in the dark and crawled into the other twin bed. She squeezed her eyes shut to hold back the silly tears that threatened to spill over—but soon she had something else to worry about.

For suddenly, without warning, Weezy started tossing and turning in her sleep, making strange, guttural sounds in her throat. Then abruptly she jerked upright to a sitting position and let out a heartfelt wail, "No-o-o!

"No, no, no," she screamed at the top of her lungs. "Stop! Have you no mercy? Leave him alone! I beg you—*leave him alone!*"

She was sobbing hysterically now, as terrified Phoebe snapped on the bedside lamp. Tears were streaming down her aunt's cheeks. Throwing back the covers, she ran to her, put her arms around her and held her close. "Shh-hh," she whispered, rocking her gently back and forth. "It's okay, Weezy, honey. Everything's fine. Wake up. Oh, please, wake up!"

After a few moments Weezy's eyes snapped open. She seemed confused. "Wha—what is it?" she asked puzzled. "What's wrong? What did I do?"

"Nothing," Phoebe assured her. "I just think you were having a bad dream, that's all. You kept begging someone to stop. Does that ring a bell?"

"Oh, God! I was telling him to stop, you say? Unfortunately that would be Colonel Schatgstaff, I'm afraid."

"Colonel who?"

"Schatgstaff. His official title was Standartenfuhrer Schatgstaff or Colonel Schatgstaff. He was a high German officer in the SS—the Schutzstaffel—a much feared army unit in Nazi Germany. The Storm Troopers, as they were called, slaughtered hundreds of thousands of innocent men, women, and children before the Allies defeated Hitler and finally won the Second World War."

"And this colonel was one of them?"

Weezy nodded. "Schatgstaff was noted for his torture techniques."

Torture techniques? What next? Phoebe thought.

"The Colonel deprived his victims of food and water, I'm told, and wouldn't let them sleep, made them stand for hours on end. He pulled out their fingernails and hung them from the ceiling by their wrists, while he beat on the soles of their feet with metal truncheons. Worse, he hooked electrical wires to their genitals and systematically broke their bones and teeth."

"God!" Phoebe shuddered. "What a beast! Where'd you meet such a person?"

"I didn't," Weezy said, looking embarrassed. "He's just someone I heard about a long time ago, who scared me. You know how some children fantasize about a boogeyman in the closet? Well, Colonel Schatgstaff is my grown-up boogeyman, that's all. I haven't thought of him in ages. But lately, it's strange, he's been coming back more and more to haunt my dreams—I don't know why. But I'm sorry if I frightened you, honey."

"That's okay," Phoebe said. "I guess everyone's entitled to a bad dream now and then."

"Well, thank you for understanding. You're a sweetheart."

"Oh, I don't know about that," Phoebe told her. She kissed her aunt's cheek, then released her. She went back to her own bed, convinced she'd never get to sleep.

44

Chapter Seven

The next thing she knew Weezy was gently shaking her shoulders, telling her to rise and shine, even though it was still dark outside the window.

"What time is it?" she asked groggily.

"Five-thirty," Weezy said. "I'd like to be on the road by six, if you think you can make it."

"Sure. Fine," Phoebe said, struggling up out of the mists of sleep. A shower restored her physically. But the sadness was still there when she remembered the less-than-ideal conditions under which she and Cody had parted the night before. Nevertheless she made herself get on the ball and was dressed, packed, ready to go in less than half-an-hour.

Picking up their bags she and Weezy went out into the deserted lobby, only to find a chain across the front door. "What in the world—?" Weezy shook the chain vigorously. "Why I do believe we're locked in."

"No way," Phoebe said. She, too, rattled the chain a couple of times, but nothing happened. She glanced around. Although the lobby was lighted no one was on the desk. A sign over the dining room said, Open at Seven. For one mad moment she wondered—actually dared hoped—that Cody had done this to keep them from leaving. Then she discarded that notion as just too silly. Fifteen minutes passed with the two of them alternately pulling and yanking on the chain to no avail.

"I guess we'll just have to wait until someone gets up and unlocks the chain for us," Phoebe said.

Weezy sighed. "Looks that way. I was planning on getting to Denver before lunch, but the way things are going—oh, dear!" Suddenly clutching her chest she slumped over. Then half-staggering, she groped her way to the nearest chair and flopped down.

Alarmed, Phoebe rushed to help her. "What's wrong?"

"Nuh-nothing," Weezy said. "I'm all right."

"Are you sure?"

"Positive." Weezy nodded. "Guess I'm just a little more tired than I realized." She looked awfully pale, but she managed a smile.

Frightened, Phoebe turned back to the door, concentrating hard on the problem. Suddenly she saw something that had escaped her notice before. "Weezy, look—am I nuts or is that a key hanging on the wall? Do you suppose—? I'm going to try it."

She put the key in the lock at the end of the chain, turned, and violà the chain opened. But by now she knew something was definitely wrong with her aunt. Weezy was still half-sprawled in the chair, her face white, but she'd opened her pillbox and was popping pills into her mouth. She obviously no longer gave a hoot as to whether Phoebe saw what she was doing or not, and she no longer seemed in any hurry to leave. Instead she was murmuring something about Inspiration Peaks being such a lovely spot. "Why don't we stay a while longer? What are we rushing off for?"

"Beats me," Phoebe said, relieved to see a hint of color returning to her aunt's face. "I'd like to stay, but I thought you wanted to get to Denver as soon as possible to see Gram and Franny, meet the new baby."

"Oh, I do, I do! Nothing's going to keep me from holding that precious bundle in my arms. But I'll call Jenna, tell her we're going to be a little late, that's all. Now help me back to the room, will you, honey?"

"Sure," Phoebe said, glancing out the lodge window. At just that moment she noticed Cody driving into the yard in his pickup, and her heart gave such a leap into her throat it almost choked her.

But when they got back to the room she wondered again if something was seriously wrong with her aunt. Worried, she suggested they call a doctor.

"I don't need a doctor," Weezy insisted. "I just need a little rest, that's all. Then I'll be fit as a fiddle. I think I just got tuckered out from all the running around I've been doing lately."

Running around? Phoebe lifted an eyebrow. "Golly, I didn't know you were such a swinger," she said.

Weezy smiled. "Well, I'd hardly call myself a swinger, but something is going on in Santa Fe every minute if you're social. And you know what they say, 'There's no fool like an old fool,' or something similarly profound. Anyway I need a day or two to catch my breath and I'll be fine, but I don't want to cramp your style." She regarded Phoebe with a look of tender amusement. "Why don't you find that nice young man and see what he's up to this morning."

"Well, I could I suppose," Phoebe said, blushing. "It might be fun."

"I'd guarantee it," Weezy assured her with a wink. "So be off with you." She gave Phoebe's backside a playful swat.

A short time later, after some searching, she did find Cody down at the stable. He was surrounded by twelve or fifteen people, both adults and kids, eagerly vying for his attention. When he saw her, his face lit up, like a switch had been turned on inside. "You came back! I can't believe it," he marveled.

Phoebe laughed. "Actually we never went away. Believe it or not there was a chain across the front door this morning and we couldn't get out. Then when I finally figured out how to unlock the darn thing my aunt wasn't feeling so hot, and she decided we ought to stay a little longer. So-o—" she put out her hands, "—here I am."

"Well, say, that's a dang shame about your aunt, such a nice lady, but your staying is the best news I've heard in ages," he told her. And the way he was beaming looked like he meant it. But he was so busy helping to get a party ready for riding he didn't have time to talk much.

As one of the wranglers called off each person's name and the name of the horse he or she would be riding, Cody came forward to help the rider mount and adjust the stirrups. Even in worn work clothes and the battered old boots he was wearing this morning, he looked better than any ordinary human being had a right to look, Phoebe thought. His back was arrow straight, and his light hair gleamed golden in the sun, where it peeked out from under the Western straw hat he was wearing. When he bent over to give someone a leg up, she noticed how the muscles of his thighs pulled against his jeans. She felt a mysterious wetness between her legs.

"Want to join us on the trail ride?" he asked her, over his shoulder. "We'll only be gone for an hour or two, and it's nothing too strenuous."

"Why, thanks, I'd like that," Phoebe said. "Only I'm not the world's best rider. I wouldn't want to hold anyone back."

Cody seemed to find that vastly amusing. He moved closer to whisper in her ear, "Believe me, you won't hold anyone back. Most of these folks are tenderfoots. Can't you tell? Besides I've got the perfect horse for you."

He went in the stable and came back leading a pretty gray mare named Primrose, which he soon had saddled and bridled. He gave Phoebe a hand up, and then they were off, an older wrangler named Jill in the lead, Cody bringing up the rear, with Phoebe right in front of him.

They went down the road single file and crossed a small bridge over a creek, then started up one of the many trails through the woods. It was a truly glorious morning, the sun angling through the trees, evaporating the morning dew, and intensifying the fragrance in the air. They went through an aspen grove, green and quivering, and a stretch of tall, dark pines. Soon the trail started getting steeper and rockier.

Phoebe had no idea where they were going and was a little nervous at first. But she noticed how carefully Primrose picked her way through the rocks, so she soon relaxed and gave the horse its head. Cody kept talking to her as though they were the only two people on the trail.

"You sure you haven't done a lot of riding?"

"Not much," Phoebe said. "Oh, I used to ride sometimes in the summer in Evergreen, where my aunt had a vacation cabin. My aunt's friend would rent horses in the village and take my sister and me riding, which we loved. But we never stayed in Evergreen more than a few weeks at a time, so I didn't get in much practice."

Their mother would never let them stay longer than that, she remembered, even though they'd beg her every year. "What do you see in that place?" Mrs. Fox used to ask them. "There's absolutely *nothing* to do there. I hated it when I was a child. Used to have a real fit when Mom would force me to stay at Aunt Weezy's cabin in the summer. I caused such a ruckus, when I got to high school, she finally told Weezy that nothing would make me go up there anymore."

But that had never been the case with her and Franny, Phoebe thought, and the twins, Alex and Jack, loved the little cabin, too.

"Does your aunt still have her place in Evergreen?" Cody asked.

"No." Phoebe shook her head sadly. "She sold it around the same time she sold her apartment in New York. It was just before she went into this assisted-living place in Santa Fe, so I haven't been riding in, oh, gosh, it must be two or three years."

"Yeah? Well, you sure haven't forgotten how to sit on a horse, let me tell you. I'd hire you as a hand on my ranch any day—if I had a ranch, that is."

Phoebe smiled. "You'll have one someday I bet."

"How you figure? I'm poor, gal."

"If you go to college and get a degree and save your money, who knows—you could buy a right nice spread, I bet."

He laughed. "Don't hold your breath." But when she turned her head to smile at him he looked pleased, she noticed, and his eyes sparkled.

As for herself, she was having such a good time, she never wanted it to end. Leaning back in the saddle, she took pleasure in the gentle rocking motion of the horse and watched a hawk circling lazily in the azure sky. The trail continued upward for several miles, weaving through strands of blue spruce and conifer, while in the distance majestic mountains lifted snow-capped peaks into the sky.

The trail went up, up, up, where it divided, and then they started down, crossing meadows filled with columbine and Indian paintbrush. All too soon they were back on the dirt road leading to the stable.

Back at the resort, Cody slid from the saddle and reaching up gave Phoebe a hand to help her to the ground. "Did you like that? Wasn't it fun?"

"Terrific." She nodded. But her legs were so stiff she could hardly walk.

Cody took one look at her ungainly gait and immediately sized up the situation. "That's what happens to some folks when they haven't been on a horse for a spell. Now what you should do," he told her, "is go straight to the bathhouse and take a soak."

"Good idea," Phoebe murmured. "I'll do that."

"And say, after you get yourself unkinked," he added, "do you think I could see you tonight? We could go dancing again—or whatever."

"I'd like that." Her smile was radiant. "But I'll have to check with my aunt first, see how she's feeling, you know?"

"Sure. But I bet it'll be all right with her. She's one nice lady, that aunt of yours."

Chapter Eight

"Of course, sweetie," Weezy said, when Phoebe broached the subject. "Go! Have fun. I don't need you."

"Are you sure?"

"Positive. I told you, all I need is a little rest. I already feel a hundred percent better than I did this morning."

And she did look better, Phoebe thought, with her color back to normal, her blue eyes as warm and shining as ever. Maybe that's why, as they got ready for dinner, she decided to confide in her; she wanted to get her aunt's reaction.

So as she stood before the mirror combing her hair, she said ever so casually, "You know I've been thinking—since I won't be living in New York next year I might go to C.U. like the rest of the family. Assuming I can get in, of course."

"Now why wouldn't you get in?" Weezy smiled. "Smart cookie like you? I bet C. U. would love to have you. But would a certain young man with yellow hair have anything to do with this sudden interest in Boulder?"

"It might," Phoebe admitted, dropping her eyes. "He's so cool—I can't believe he really likes me, but he seems to."

"And why wouldn't he like you?" Weezy asked. She came up beside her then and put her hands on Phoebe's shoulders. "Take a good look at yourself and tell me—is that girl in the glass anything to sneeze at?"

Phoebe glanced in the mirror and did a double take. Where had the pouting, unhappy creature who'd stared back at her in the Albuquerque restroom just a few days before disappeared to? The girl in the mirror tonight, by some strange alchemy she didn't understand, was radiant, glowing.

This new girl looked confident, too, as if nothing could faze her. When they walked into the dining room a short time later, Cody's eyes told her he thought she was pretty special.

"Good evening, ladies," he said, a little shyly, as he pulled out Weezy's chair.

"Good evening, Cody," Weezy said, her keen eyes taking in his freshly washed jeans, his crisp blue-and-white striped shirt. "My, how nice you look this evening."

He blushed. "Thank you, ma'am."

"Are you going to see to it that my niece has a good time tonight?"

"I'm going to do my best."

"Then you'll succeed. I guarantee it."

They all laughed, and Cody took their orders. When he'd gone to the kitchen, Weezy asked, "Where are you going tonight?"

Phoebe sighed and wrinkled her nose. "The Roundup, I suppose."

"Anything wrong with the Roundup?"

Phoebe shook her head. "It's okay. Only trouble is his sister works there. Her name's Wynonna, and she's pretty possessive. She raised him and she thinks she owns him. Last night, to ditch her, we had to crawl out of the place on our hands and knees—literally."

"That doesn't sound like much fun."

"Cody's a wonderful dancer."

"Sounds to me like that young man's a wonderful everything."

"Mmm-mm," Phoebe said, blushing.

"But the Roundup's still not your idea of a great date, I take it? You'd like to go someplace a little spiffier maybe?"

"Sort of. Is that awful of me?"

"Certainly not. It's normal. Remember that young man I was

telling you about who had the apartment upstairs from mine during the war?"

"Sure. Mickey McGuire," Phoebe said instantly.

"You remembered." Weezy looked pleased.

How could I forget, the way you went on and on about him? "He was doing something at NYU; right? Had to do with Intelligence?"

"Correct." Weezy nodded. "It was very secretive, of course, and he couldn't tell me much about it. Not that I didn't try to find out everything I could," she added, laughing . . .

* * *

"So where do you think they'll send you when you finish the course?" she asked him as they sat in the garden.

He surprised her by answering, "Oh, someplace in England directed by British Intelligence, I imagine. Chances are I'll probably be assigned to an airborne division."

"Oh, dear." Weezy shivered. "That sounds scary. Are you scared?"

"A little," he admitted, "but it's what I signed up for. My German's pretty good, and it's the best way I could think of to get to Germany, hopefully hook up with Otto again."

"Who's Otto?"

"My first cousin, and also my best friend. Remember I told you my mom came from Germany and that she'd won a scholarship to Julliard?"

"I remember," Weezy said. "But she didn't return to Germany when she graduated, did she?"

"No." He shook his head. "In the meantime she met my dad, who was a student at Columbia at the time, and they got married and eventually settled in Kansas, in Dad's hometown. But my mom loved Germany and her family there, and she used to go back every summer to visit and she'd take me with her. We always stayed with her brother Bertram, who worked for the government and had a son named Otto, who was just my age.

"Otto was a really great guy," he added, smiling, "very smart and savvy, even as a kid, and completely different than his old man, who always followed the straight and narrow. Actually Bertram was something of a prig, no other way to describe him, but my mom loved him because he was her brother. So she tended to overlook certain things, such as what was happening in Germany."

"And what about you?" Weezy asked. "How did you feel about it?"

"Me?" He shrugged. "I'm almost ashamed to say it, but I was completely apolitical at that stage of my life. I didn't know what was going on and couldn't have cared less. I just loved every minute I spent with Otto, he was such fun to be around. We'd swim in a nearby lake, go on long hikes in the mountains, and think up nutty things to do to impress the girls, whom we were just becoming aware of. But after the Nazis came to power, everything changed. At fifteen Otto joined the Hitler Youth."

"The Hitler Youth!" Weezy exclaimed. "For heaven's sake, why?"

Mickey smiled wryly. "Don't look so shocked. For a lot of young Germans at the time it seemed like the natural thing to do. The Youth offered lots of excitement and camaraderie with its various programs and field trips to interesting places. It was also a way for Germany to gain respect again, Otto wrote me, with the other nations of the world."

"Respect?" Weezy said, wondering if she was missing something here. "What do you mean? When you think of the horrid things the Germans have done, the bombing of helpless cities, the slaughter of innocent civilians—"

"Right," Mickey shrugged. "Don't get me wrong. I'm not excusing any of the atrocities. But whether a person agrees or not, Germany suffered terrible humiliation after losing the First World War and the harsh conditions the Allied powers imposed on the country. The Treaty of Versailles forced the Germans to accept sole responsibility for starting the war, and as punishment they had to give up territories and pay a huge sum in war damages, called *reparations*. The German people were tired of the poverty and poor living conditions and wanted a strong leader—hence Hitler and the rise of the National Socialist Party, the Nazis. Hitler gave them hope, the promise of better days, don't you see? I don't think a lot of Germans realized what they were getting into. Like my mom. She buried her head in the sand for a long time."

"In what way?" Weezy asked.

"Well," Mickey hesitated, then said slowly, "Mom's family had a maid named Esther. She was more a member of the family than a servant since she practically brought up my mom and her brother after their mother died. She loved them like her own, and they felt the same about her. After my grandfather passed away my uncle Bertram, who by then had married and had Otto, moved into the old family home, and Esther continued to run things. I always looked forward to seeing her every summer, and so did Mom. Esther was such a kind, jolly, all-around good person.

"But one year when we got to Germany for our annual visit," he continued, his voice shaded with regret, "Esther was gone. Mom was puzzled and upset. When she asked Uncle Bertram what had happened, he seemed embarrassed and was evasive. He finally broke down and told her the truth. He said that since the Nazis had come to power they'd passed a lot of new laws, such as no gentile family could hire a Jew to work in their home, and although the family had never given it a thought Esther's last name was Levi. Well, of course Mom was outraged and berated Bertram for treating dear Esther in such a shabby fashion, but he said he had no choice. Bertram had been a midlevel functionary in the government for years without much chance of advancement. After he joined the Nazis, he became a rising star. He was proud of his position in the Third Reich and told Mom he couldn't do anything to jeopardize his career, such as openly defying one of the Nazi edicts, and surely she could understand that. He said he felt bad about Esther, too, but she was okay. He'd given her a generous severance allowance for all her years of dedicated work for the family, and she'd gone back to her home in Bavaria. Well, Mom was still upset and not satisfied with Bertram's explanation, but she loved her brother so she let it ride."

"And did you let it ride, too?" Weezy asked, not even bothering to hide her astonishment.

"Yep." He shrugged, his face a gamut of conflicting emotions. "Don't get me wrong. I liked Esther and missed her, but I accepted Uncle Bertram's assurance that she was okay. And I was having a great time with Otto, who seemed to enjoy being a member of the Hitler Youth. But by the time we returned the next summer, our last summer in Germany, incidentally—Otto's eyes had been opened. I don't know what brought about the change, maybe a variety of things, but it was one-hundred percent genuine, I know that. By age sixteen he no longer wanted any part of the Hitler Youth and tried to resign, but Uncle Bertram wouldn't let him. Otto didn't know where to turn, even though he despised the Nazis and saw them for what they are…. '*Ich hasse alles!*' he used to tell me privately. 'I hate them all! Master race? *Quatsch!* Rubbish! All those goose-stepping bullies make me sick,' he declared."

"But he still went along with it?" Weezy asked.

Mickey said sadly, "As I told you, he had no choice. He was just a kid. What could he do? It was different with my mom. Her best friend growing up was a beautiful girl named Leah Friedman, whom Bertram had had a crush on in high school. But Leah was a Jew. One day she and her whole family just disappeared, even though her father had won the Iron Cross for bravery during the first World War. I remember how upset my mom was when she went to Leah's house and couldn't find her. Another family had moved into the house and they wouldn't talk. So Mom asked Uncle Bertram for help. He investigated and told her the family had been put under protective custody, 'relocated', he called it, for their own good. Well, that finally did it for my mom. That afternoon she packed up our things and we returned to the States. I never saw Otto again."

"But didn't you write, keep in touch?"

"Oh, for a while we wrote letters. But in '39, as you know, Germany invaded Poland, and soon the war started. So I'm hoping that when the war ends—" his mouth tightened "—and it will eventually, somehow I'll find Otto again."

"I'm sure you will," Weezy said. Anxious to change the subject because he seemed so unhappy, she added, "So what shall we do tonight, soldier? Got any brilliant ideas?"

He laughed and looked pleased. "As a matter of fact I do. My friend Rudy Diels, whom I want you to meet—you'll like him— talked me into a crap game last night and miracle of miracles, I won the pot. So I thought we might have dinner at the Promenade Café in Rockefeller Center. I hear it's a very nice restaurant. Best of all, there's a skating rink right in front. So we could rent you a pair of skates—"

"No need," she said instantly. "I brought my skates."

"Honest?" he laughed. "Then let's go!"

"Okay," she said. She ran to her room and got out her white figure skates, which she'd pushed to the back of the closet, since she hadn't expected to do any skating in Manhattan. As a matter of fact she didn't really know why she'd even brought the skates with her—as well as one of her old skating costumes, a two-piece outfit in blue velvet with a short skirt lined in white satin. But something had told her that she might have a chance to skate again, and obviously her intuition was right, she thought, as she happily changed her clothes.

"Wow!" Mickey said, when he saw her, his whole face lighting up. "Golly, you look sensational!"

"Thank you, sir." She curtsied and gave him a big smile. But inside she was thinking, since she hadn't practiced in a long time, *Dear God, please don't let me fall flat on my face.*

They took a taxi to the restaurant since Mickey was feeling so flush, but to her disappointment he told her he wasn't going to skate with her. He said, to be honest, he didn't really know how, so he was just going to get a ringside table, order a drink, and enjoy seeing her perform.

"Well, I'll do my best." She laughed, as she laced up her skates. "But don't expect too much. Remember, I haven't skated in ages. And you never know," she added worried.

But he assured her she'd do just fine, and leaning down, kissed the tip of her nose. Then surprising her, as he often did, he suddenly quoted: "I have no life but this, / To lead it here / Nor any Death / but less Dispelled from there."

Delighted she joined in, finishing the stanza with him: "Nor tie to Earth to come, / Nor action new / Except through this Extent / The love of you."

"So you know Emily Dickinson?" she said, amazed that he liked poetry in addition to all his other attributes.

"Yep. Miss Dickinson is one of my favorite poets," he confessed with a broad smile. "I love the cadence and the passion of her words. But I didn't really appreciate them until I met you. And now—"

"And now?" she teased him.

"Well, it confirms what I've suspected since the first time I saw you. You and I are indisputably on the same wavelength, sweet girl. Now get out there and do your stuff."

"Yes, sir." She laughed, and lost no time going out on the ice.

Her legs did feel a little wobbly at first, no doubt about that, but after a few times around the rink she regained her confidence and started enjoying herself. She listened to the music blaring over the loudspeaker and set up a steady rhythm as she changed from inside to outside edges and experimented with a few basic turns. After successfully completing a *mohawk*, a two-foot turn, then a *choctaw*, a one-footer, which was a little more difficult, she decided to increase her diversity by doing one of her favorite moves, the spiral. With one leg high in the air, pointing skyward, she smiled happily at Mickey, and from there executed a couple of spread eagles, both inside and outside. Next she did a forward lunge, then went into a series of spins, going faster with each variation.

Keeping her standing leg straight she went into a basic scratch spin, followed by a back scratch. Next was an impressive sit spin, both forward and backward, and a forward *camel*, where she sprang into the air, swinging her right leg in a wide arc to the side, while her left leg swung in an arc to the back. For a split second she seemed to hang in the air, which brought a burst of applause from Mickey and some of the other spectators seated at the ringside tables, and increased her confidence. So exercising her creativity, and for the sheer joy of it, she tried a few jumps. She was soaring a few feet off the ice, but failed to look behind her and crashed into another skater, a man, knocking him down.

Embarrassed and apologetic, she rushed to the man's side to do what she could, only to be pushed aside by a short, stubby fellow in an ill-fitting suit. "Are you hurt, sir? Let me help you," this fellow said to the man who'd fallen, who was already getting to his feet.

"No, I'm okay, Jenkins," the man told his would-be helper as he shooed him off. "Go back to the table. I'll call you if I need you."

"Gosh, sir, I'm so sorry," Weezy said, only to have the man brush off her apology.

"Don't worry about it, miss. I'm fine," he said, smiling down at her. He was extremely tall and very good looking, with an intelligent, fine-featured face, and an unmistakable twinkle in his eyes. "It was really my fault for getting too close," he continued, "but I was impressed with your performance. I must say, young lady, you'd give my friend, Sonja Henie, a run for the money."

"Sonja Henie? Ohmigod!" Weezy cried, both hands flying to her mouth. The Norwegian figure skater and Olympic champion had long been an idol of hers. "You know Sonja Henie?" she said, awestruck.

"Yes, I see her quite often in Sun Valley when I go on vacation. Like you, she's a joy to watch. And you know," he added thoughtfully, his eyes crinkling at the corners, "you're not only a fine skater, but you look amazingly like the actress Teresa Wright. Anyone ever tell you that?"

"I think she does, too," Mickey, who had come up beside them, said. "Only, in my opinion, my girl's better looking."

The man laughed. "Spoken like a true connoisseur of good looks—or a young man in love."

Then he turned to the fellow in the ill-fitting suit, who was now clutching his arm desperately. "We really must go, sir," the fellow implored him. "The photographers from *Life* magazine and Miss Wright are waiting—"

"All right, Jenkins, all right," the man said. But before leaving he turned his attention back to Weezy and added, "Goodbye, my dear. It's been a real pleasure meeting you. Good luck in the future, whether on or off the ice."

"Thank you." Weezy smiled. And after watching the two men walk off, she turned to Mickey and said, "Golly, what a nice gentleman. Can't say the same for that pushy guy with him, though. What do you suppose his job is anyway? Some kind of bodyguard you think?"

Mickey shook his head. "More likely he's someone from Public Relations."

"Public Relations?" Weezy said puzzled.

"Sure." Mickey nodded. "Didn't you get it when the guy said *Life* magazine and Teresa Wright were waiting?"

"What was I supposed to *get*?" Weezy asked, puzzled. "I think I've heard of Teresa Wright, but I don't know much about her."

"Well, it just so happens she's starring in *The Pride of the Yankees*, the movie that's playing at Radio City Music Hall right now. And her costar in the film—a really big star, no doubt about that—is that gentleman you were just talking to."

"That man is a movie star?" Weezy murmured astonished. "I thought he looked kind of familiar, but I can't place him. I never go to the movies anymore."

At which Mickey threw back his head and roared. "Oh, honey," he said when his voice came back, "I bet you're the only girl in America who could knock down Gary Cooper—and not even know it!"

Chapter Nine

Right after dinner Weezy retired to their room while Phoebe sat in the lobby, flipping through a magazine as she waited for Cody. Shortly after eight he finished his stint in the dining room and came out to where she was sitting.

"Ready?"

"All set," she told him, smiling. They went out to his pickup and started driving toward Buena Vista.

"The Roundup okay?" he asked.

"Sure." Then she added half-jokingly, "Only when it's time to leave, I hope we don't have to sneak out on our hands and knees to get away from your sister."

"I'll guarantee it." He laughed but looked a little shamefaced. "I know Wynonna comes across as kind of bossy at times."

Kind of bossy? That was surely the understatement of the year.

"But like I told you," Cody was saying, "we haven't had anyone else for a long time. Its made us more dependent on each other, you know?"

Maybe too dependent. "Hmm-mm. What's she going to do when you go away to college?"

'Oh, well—" he shrugged, "—that's a long way off."

"Don't classes start in September?"

"I'm not sure." He didn't seem to want to continue the

conversation, and they were at the Roundup almost before she knew it.

The moment they walked through the door, Wynonna spotted them and dropping what she was doing, rushed right over. She hugged Cody with such enthusiasm you would have thought she hadn't seen him in weeks instead of just a few hours. To Phoebe she said, "Hi, there," sounding almost friendly—until Phoebe looked in her eyes.

Between stints with her other customers she'd plop herself down at their table. Phoebe found they couldn't carry on the simplest conversation without Wynonna bringing the subject around to what she and Cody would do when they saved up a little more money. "We'll pack the pickup and head straight for California. Cal-ee-FOR-nay, here we come!" she enthused.

"And I just can't wait," she added, giving Cody's arm a squeeze. "The folks around here can just watch our dust. Right, little bro?"

"Sure, Sis," Cody drawled. "Whatever you say. But I wouldn't advise anyone to hold their breath, not the way you spend money."

Wynonna scoffed. "Oh, poo! We'll make it, sonny-boy. By the way, did you show Miss Glamorpuss here—" she winked at Phoebe, "—no offense, kid, the boots? What'd she think of 'em?"

"Don't know. Haven't asked her."

"Well, what's stopping you? Go on. Ask."

"Okay, okay, if you insist." As if to humor her, but at the same time plainly embarrassed, he stuck his feet out in front of him, clad in the same handsome cowboy boots he'd worn the night before. "Wynonna gave me these for my birthday," he told Phoebe, wiggling his toes up and down. "Only set her back five hundred."

"Dollars?" Phoebe gasped.

"You've got it." Wynonna nodded proudly. "Five hundred smackeroos. But they're worth every penny. Them there boots are gen-u-wine ostrich skin, got a paper to prove it. So what the heck? Nothing's too good for my little bro. Don't you think he'd be great in the movies?"

The movies! Was that why she wanted to go to California? Phoebe had thought maybe she wanted to search for their mother, which was understandable. But if her plan was to help Cody break into the movies that was pretty far-fetched. Didn't the silly girl know what the odds were against that?

"What about college? Cody's scholarship to Boulder?" Phoebe said.

"Oh, that." Wynonna dismissed it with a wave of her hand. "Cody's not about to take that old scholarship thing seriously. Why should he? Waste his time in stupid old Boulder for four years when he could be doing something really important?"

Like waiting on tables, hoping to be discovered? Phoebe thought. Fortunately Leroy, the bartender, called to Wynonna to get on the stick, and something in his voice must have told her he meant it. At any rate she left, but Phoebe knew she'd be back.

Cody asked her to dance. As she went into his arms she said, trying to keep her voice light, "I take it your sister doesn't think much of higher education? What's she got against college anyway?"

"Oh, she hasn't got anything against it. She just feels you can get along without it."

She drew back and looked at him. "You don't feel that way, do you?"

He shrugged. "Ah, I don't know. Wynonna's been on her own since she was fifteen, like I told you. And she's done all right for herself."

If you call working in a two-bit bar "all right". That thought immediately popped into her head. Ashamed, she said, "It must have been hard on her though, having to quit school and go to work at such an early age."

"Nah." Cody shook his head. "She hated school. Not that she was dumb or anything," he added quickly. "But she had a gosh-awful time with her reading. She got her letters all mixed up, saw things backwards. They got a name for it now—"

"Dyslexia?"

"Right. These days they can help kids with that kind of problem.

63

But when Wynonna was little, nobody knew what was wrong. Our folks moved around a lot, which didn't help. One year we went to five different schools, and the teachers always thought Wynonna was stupid. After a while she kind of thought so herself. How could she help it? Anyway, she wasn't sorry to quit school and go to work."

"That's a very sad story," Phoebe said.

"Yeah. But my sister hates pity. More'n anything just about."

Not more than me, I bet. But she could live with that, as long as Cody liked her. And there wasn't much doubt about that.

"Hey, you're one cool dancer," he shouted in her ear a little later.

"You, too," she shouted back. They had to shout to be heard the music was suddenly so loud and raucous.

"Man, it's sure noisy in here tonight," Cody complained. "Or is it just my imagination?"

"It's noisy," Phoebe agreed. "I wish we could go someplace quiet and talk."

"That makes two of us. Got any suggestions?"

"Well-ll." She took a deep breath and let it out slowly, wondering if what she was thinking was a really dumb idea. But saying it anyway. "You could always show me where you live."

"What?" He seemed stunned. "You mean it? You really want to see my old trailer?"

"Why not?" She felt she'd been given a second chance, and she intended to make the most of it. "We can't hear ourselves think in here. Besides, I've never been inside a trailer.'"

"No kidding?"

"No kidding. It will be a whole new experience."

"Then let's go." He grabbed her hand and started for the door. "Before you change your mind."

Phoebe laughed. "I won't change my mind." But as they ran to the pickup she could feel the butterflies dancing in her stomach, and the palms of her hands were wet.

The drive didn't take long and she wondered again how smart

this was, but pushed the thought from her. At first impression the trailer, a square, boxy-looking structure near a creek in the little town of Nathrop, didn't have a whole lot to recommend it. One of several in a trailer park, it was indistinguishable from its neighbors, except for a small, well-manicured yard in front filled with masses of white petunias.

"What's that heavenly smell?" Phoebe asked as they started up the walk.

Cody smiled. "Wynonna's flowers. Aren't they something?"

"I never knew flowers smelled that sweet before."

"It's 'cause they're all white," he told her. "In colored flowers the perfume goes to the color, Wynonna says. But in the white ones it's concentrated, so you get it all."

He opened the door and flicked on the overhead lights. "Well, here we are. Come on in."

Phoebe glanced quickly around: white walls, chintz curtains at a picture window and a studio couch covered in gay red and blue plaid.

"This here's the living room," Cody was saying. "And right over here—" he took a few steps to the left, "—is the kitchen where Wynonna whips up some mighty fine grub, let me tell you. Now you want to see something different?" He moved forward again. "I got the idea from an article in *Popular Mechanics*. If you push the back of this bench, see?" He demonstrated. "The bench goes down, and you've got yourself a table or a desk. Pretty neat, huh?"

"Really neat." Phoebe smiled. "Did you build all this furniture yourself?"

"Most of it. Wynonna made all the curtains and slipcovers. The stuff Mama left us was all kind of falling apart, so we've done a little redecorating—when we had the dough."

"Well, you've got yourself quite a place here," Phoebe said as they walked down the hall.

"Thanks," he said. "We like it."

There were two small bedrooms in back with a bath between. Cody's bedroom, the smaller of the two, had a king-size bed that took up most of the floor. There was also a straight-back chair in the room and a dresser pushed up against one wall, with a CD player on top and a stack of CD's beside it.

"Say, what kind of music do you like to make out to?" Cody asked. He sounded very off-hand, but Phoebe noticed that his Adam's apple was bobbing.

"I don't know," she said, swallowing hard. "I've never made out with anyone."

"What? You're putting me on."

"No, I'm serious. I was always too busy for guys. I studied dancing for years and was always taking lessons, practicing, and performing in recitals. Dance was my whole life."

"Doesn't sound like much fun."

"No, it was real hard work, but that's the way I wanted it." Almost shyly she told him of how she'd dreamed of becoming a prima ballerina —and how crushed she'd been when she failed the audition and the dream came crashing down.

"I thought I was pretty hot stuff. Everyone in town said I was, and I believed them, dumb me. So it was a terrible shock being passed over. I wanted to die." She bit her lip. "I almost did."

"And now?" he asked gently.

"It still hurts. It always will, I expect. But I know everyone can't be a star, and I'll learn to live with it. My aunt Weezy knows something about disappointment, and she says it gets easier after a while. I hope she's right."

"Well, hey, you'll always be a star in my book," Cody said. He picked up a CD from the stack, put it in the player, and suddenly the glorious strains of Prokofiev's Third Piano Concerto began drifting through the little room.

Phoebe was stunned. "Where'd you get that music?"

"You like it?" He was watching her intently.

"Yes, it's one of my favorites. But I didn't expect to hear it here, that's all. I had you pegged as more—"

"The country and western type?" He grinned wryly. "Well, I like country, can't pretend I don't. I'm a big Garth Brooks fan. But

I love classical music. I had a teacher in high who played the great composers in study hall every day. He'd tell us little stories about them to whet our appetites."

"What kind of stories?" She was fascinated.

"Well, the obvious, of course. Like Beethoven's Ninth was composed when he was stone deaf, and Franz Schubert, of the lovely lieder, died of a social disease. And did you know Thomas Arne was plagued with indigestion so fierce it ruined his disposition, and Franz Liszt was a regular randy-dandy? Or that Gustav Mahler composed nine symphonies but was afraid to tackle a tenth? He started Number Ten but he was so superstitious, he couldn't complete it. He was afraid he'd die if he did." He grinned again. "I could go on and on, but you get the picture. Mr. Atkins, that was the teacher's name, gave us a little spice to make the composers seem human and then, when we were interested, he played their music, that incredible music, and we were hooked."

"Smart man," Phoebe said. "Where's Mr. Atkins now?"

"He died last year and left me all his CD's. His death was a real tragedy. The poor guy was only thirty-three."

"I'm so sorry. What did he die of?"

"AIDS."

"AIDS? Even out here?"

"Everywhere."

"I'm sorry," she said again, and was surprised to find her eyes were wet.

"Thanks," Cody said, reaching for her hand. Slowly he pulled her to him, and they started dancing.

The space was so confining he had to hold her close, even closer than he'd held her in the Roundup. Her head was on his shoulder, and she could feel his long legs pressing into hers, feel the warmth of his body through his clothes. And she wondered again how his body would look without clothes, how his bare skin would feel under her hands. The thought made her so dizzy, she stumbled.

"Sorry," she apologized. "Didn't mean to step on your toes."

"You didn't. You're a fantastic dancer."

"Not tonight, I'm afraid."

"Every night. I bet you'd be fantastic in other ways, too. Do you think—is it possible we could explore that?"

Explore it? She could feel the blood rushing to her face and swallowed again. "I—I don't know," she said, catching her breath. She pulled away and went over to stand behind the straight-back chair. Leaning her elbows on the top she did a few pliés, out of habit. The butterflies in her stomach had gotten completely out of hand now. No matter how many deep breaths she took she couldn't calm down. Her hands were trembling, and her mouth was so dry she could hardly get the words out.

"You—you know what to do, I suppose—so that nothing happens?"

"I know what to do." He put out his hand, stroked the top of her hand with one finger. "It'll be safe. You don't have to worry."

"I'm not worried. I trust you."

"Thank you. You're sure one swell girl, Phoebe Fox." Reaching out, he drew her to him again. But this time they gave up all pretense of dancing. They stood holding each other, his cheek against hers, her heart beating fast. Then her arms, seemingly of their own accord, wrapped around his neck, and she could feel a most delicious warmth creeping up her arms and down her legs, enveloping her in its soft cocoon.

He had one hand on her waist and with the other hand stroked her cheek, her neck, her hair. "I love your hair. It's so pretty, like sunshine on water. Oh, Phoebe, Phoebe—" he buried his face in it "—a guy could drown in such hair."

He was holding both her hands in his now, holding them close against his chest. Then he bent his head and kissed her, a soft, lingering kiss that seemed to go on forever. By the time they came up for air, Phoebe discovered they were sitting on the bed, and she wasn't sure how they got there.

"Don't be afraid," he said, his voice thick.

"I'm not afraid." The back of her neck began to tingle, but she lifted her head and looked straight into his eyes.

"I'm just dying to hold you, touch you. But if I touch you someplace you don't like, if it hurts—tell me, and I'll stop. I promise."

"All right. But—" she blinked in the harsh overhead light "—can we turn that thing off?"

"I've got a good idea." He got up from the bed and walked to the dresser, opened the top drawer. He took out a fat, stubby white candle in a green glass holder. "I won this shooting clay ducks at the Glenwood fair last year," he told her. "Cost me ten bucks, and I never had a notion what to do with it. It's supposed to be scented." He struck a match and lit the candle. The flame fluttered a few seconds in the still air and almost went out. Then it caught, and the flame pointed straight upward. "How's that?" he asked, snapping off the overhead light. "Better?"

"Much," Phoebe said. It was perfect, suddenly dark and mysterious, romantic. The darkness hid the shabby little room, and she could see his shadow on the wall as he eased out of his jeans and started putting on a condom.

She sat on the side of the bed and listened to the concerto, heard the moths attracted by the flame, battering themselves helplessly against the window screen. She smelled the woodsy scent of the candle all mixed in with the perfume from Wynonna's petunias and felt light-headed, almost giddy. *Is this me?* she wondered. *Am I really going through with this?* Would she even know what to do? Suppose he was disappointed in her? Was it too late to call the whole thing off?

She opened her mouth to say something. But then, in what seemed like no time at all, he was coming back to the bed, sitting down beside her. He put his hands on her shoulders and she had never seen such a look on a man's face. "Beautiful," he said. "You're so beautiful, honey girl. I never dreamed—" His voice broke and suddenly he caught her to him, his arms holding her tight.

She buried her face in his chest, and her nervousness went away. She felt safe of a sudden, the safest she'd ever felt in her life. After a while he laid her head back against the pillows very gently and started taking off her dress, and she helped him. She was in a fever of impatience suddenly and thought they'd never get the darn thing over her head, but soon her dress and her undies joined his in a little heap on the floor.

He started kissing her then, her eyes, her lips, and her throat and very carefully started to explore her. He ran his hands up and down her sides and touched her in places she hardly knew existed, but nothing he did hurt or frightened her. She didn't ask him to stop. Instead, after a moment's hesitation, she touched him back and heard him groan, and his naked body, bending above her, was more thrilling than she'd ever dreamed possible. He kissed her everywhere as she trembled beneath his hands, and there was a moment when she seemed to hear her heart beating very loud and fast. Just before he entered her, which was a mixture of pain and pleasure that transported her into a realm she had never imagined, she whispered, "Oh, Cody, Cody—I feel so strange. What in the world's happening to us?"

"Don't know for sure," he said, his voice so slurred she could hardly hear him. "But I think they call it falling in love."

Chapter Ten

The next day was a repeat of the day before. Weezy looked a lot better, but she seemed in no hurry to leave Mount Princeton. "It's so pleasant here," she said when they finished breakfast.

Phoebe smiled. "Can't argue with that." She could hardly wait to see Cody again, but she was prepared to spend the whole day with her aunt, until Weezy shooed her off.

"There's no point in your hanging around here, watching me read or take a nap when you could go riding with that nice young fella."

"Well, if you're sure. . ."

"I'm sure," Weezy said. "So be off with you."

"Okay." Phoebe laughed and didn't need any coaxing.

She scampered down the path to the stable and found Cody without any trouble. He was preparing some of the guests for another trail ride, and when he suggested she join them, she happily agreed.

This time he was in the lead because Jill, the other wrangler, was sick, and Phoebe was right behind him. Several obstreperous little kids were on the ride and Cody was careful to hold them in, but when they came to a fairly wide flat stretch, he let them break into a trot, then a canter.

"Low branch ahead," he called over his shoulder.

Phoebe, who had turned to watch a noisy bluejay flying

overhead, ducked just in time, but not fast enough to escape all the twigs and branches. They tore at her sweatshirt. One of the twigs barely missed her eye and lightly grazed her cheek.

"Ouch!" she cried, automatically putting a hand to her face.

Cody heard her cry and turning was beside her instantly. "Are you hurt? Let me see. Looks like you got a nasty little scratch there."

"It's nothing." She was embarrassed. "My own darn fault."

"Why, I wouldn't say that." Leaning closer impulsively he put an arm around her and gave her a hug, right in front of everyone.

"It's okay," she told him. "I'm not hurt."

"Well, I'm glad of that." He smiled, his teeth so dazzlingly bright against the tanned face, she almost lost her breath. The two top buttons of his blue work shirt were open, and she could see the sheen of perspiration on his bare chest. The muscles in his forearms flexed as he pulled on the reins.

She wondered if he was remembering, as she was, what had gone on between them the night before, and a shiver of delight went through her. She gazed at him, dazed and unraveled, and only the little kids, laughing and jeering at the hug, brought her back to reality.

For the rest of the ride he kept turning to check on her, and when they got back to the stable, he told his boss he couldn't have managed without her help. She suspected that was a slight exaggeration, but she glowed nevertheless.

She had lunch with Weezy, who said she felt much better and was anxious to get back to the new best-selling book she was reading. "So why don't you take a swim?" she suggested. "You don't have to worry about me."

"Okay," Phoebe said, smiling.

She found Cody at the pools and helped him with his lifeguard duties, even giving some youngsters from Chicago a swimming lesson. And that night after dinner they talked of going to the movies but soon scuttled that plan. As though it was pre-ordained, they drove straight to his trailer, where they didn't waste any time tearing off their clothes and falling on the bed.

As before, he kissed her lips and ear and throat and ran his tongue across her belly, and she wrapped her legs around him and hung on with all her might. She was amazed at the things he did to her, and the things she did to him without a trace of guilt or embarrassment. Somehow everything seemed natural, right, as if they'd done this forever, their bodies in perfect harmony. She'd never dreamed she could feel so good, so breathtakingly alive. Nothing on this earth had ever approached the pleasure, the sheer joy of making love with Cody Moon. And something told her nothing ever would again.

* * *

For the next two days, with Weezy happily ensconced in her room, Phoebe and Cody spent all their spare time together, either riding or swimming or, more important, making love. They would make love by the hour, stopping every now and then to catch their breath, while he turned his head on the pillow and smiled at her.

She would rest her head in the hollow between his shoulder and neck while his arms encircled her, one hand in the small of her back. With his other hand he would touch her, his fingers sliding gently across her chest, outlining the circle of her breasts, steering a feathery path down her hip, along her thigh. Gently he separated her legs with his knee as she arched up eagerly to meet him, and each time they came together it was better than the time before.

Once, though, as if needing reassurance that this wasn't just some summer fling on his part, she pushed herself up on one elbow and leaning over him, gazed deep into his eyes. "Do you really and truly love me?" she whispered, feeling this was too good to be true.

"Do I really and truly love you?" He sighed. "Ah, silly girl." His hands moved to either side of her face, and he kissed her, his tongue tracing the soft outline of her mouth. "How can I convince you? I'm just a poor cowhand, but I know my own heart. And I know I'll love you always and forever. I think something brought up together. We've been blessed."

Tears filled her eyes, then started coursing down her cheeks. "Oh, Cody, I feel exactly the same." Bending down, she kissed the pulsing hollow at the base of his throat, and he caught her to him and kissed her deeply, lips and tongue claiming her mouth as his own. Her heart flew up joyously in response, and then he was inside her again, and she was conscious of nothing except a roaring in her ears and the sweet delight of his arms around her.

The next day, after more swimming and riding, she got back to the room around five to find Weezy already dressed for dinner in pretty green silk. When she complimented her on her appearance, Weezy said she felt marvelous.

"Me, too," Phoebe said, blushing. Indeed the anticipation of what was to come later that evening was almost more than she could bear. She seemed to think of nothing but Cody, and every time she did, her heart flipped over, and a tingling sensation in the pit of her stomach radiated through her. "Oh, Weezy, I just can't tell you what an awesome time I've had here," she added, hugging her arms. "It's been the most incredible experience of my whole life."

Weezy smiled. "I know, sweetie, and I'm glad for you. Sometimes the loveliest things happen in the least expected places. But I feel so peppy, I'm afraid we'll have to leave for Denver tomorrow."

"So soon?" Phoebe stared at her, stricken.

"It's been five days."

Five days! It didn't seem possible. Although in one sense she felt like she'd known Cody forever, so much still remained to discover about him.

"You'll see him again," Weezy told her, as if reading her mind.

"I know. It's just so hard saying goodbye."

"I won't argue with that," Weezy said.

A little later they went down to the dining room, and after dinner she met Cody in the lobby, as usual. She gave him the bad news right away—that they were leaving in the morning—and he said what she'd said to Weezy.

"So soon?" His face looked as woebegone as she felt, but he tried to put up a brave front. "Then we'll just have to make tonight extra special."

"Every time with you is extra special," Phoebe said, as they walked to his pickup. It was a truly beautiful evening with the Colorado moon coming over the mountains, bathing everything in silver. They got in the pickup and she snuggled against him. He put his arms around her and kissed her, and in spite of her sadness, she decided heaven couldn't be any improvement on this. Then he started the engine, and they went straight to his trailer.

They undressed and got in bed, and his hands locked against her spine, then slipped up her arms, bringing her closer. Her whole body felt sensual and alive, and as his hand touched her naked thigh, she moaned softly and parted her legs to welcome him to her. It was like a magnetic force pulling them together. As he held her in his arms, her thoughts spun, her emotions whirled, and time after time he aroused her to a feverish pitch.

She loved the tickling sensation of his body hair against her bare skin, the way his hands, ever so gently, cupped her buttocks, her breasts. Every moment they shared was precious to her, and she didn't think she'd ever get enough of him as he hugged her tight against him. She even reveled in the shared dampness of their perspiration, and when he finally rolled over beside her, keeping one arm around her waist and drawing her close to his still-warm body, she brought her hand up and stroked his cheek, the strong line of his jaw.

"I love you so-o much, " she said softly.

"Me, too." He took her hand and raised it to his lips. "That's why this is so hard. What are we going to do, honey girl? I can't bear to tell you goodbye."

She heard the pain in his voice and in spite of her own pain, tried to reassure him. "But it's not really goodbye. I mean, not for long. We'll be together again in a few months."

"Yeah? How you figure?" He had his tongue against her cheek, lightly licking her skin. "Hmm-mm, you taste so good. You know that old saying about what little girls are made of, sugar and spice and everything nice? I never believed it until I met you."

"Thanks." Phoebe laughed, the laugh ending in a catchy little hiccup. "I'm awfully glad I please you. But listen, Cody, remember how I told you my aunt Weezy and I were going to Denver to see my grandmother—and also my sister, Franny, and her new baby?"

"Yep." He kissed her, then put his face next to hers for a moment, running a hand down her hair. "But what's that got to do with us?"

"Everything. Because I know, along about Thanksgiving, maybe sooner, Mom will start working on Dad to get him to fly to Denver to see her new grandchild Although she won't admit it she's dying to see that little girl, and of course, I'll have a seat on that plane when it lands in Denver. And since you'll be in Boulder, only half an hour or so away, we can figure out lots of ways to get together. Then come January—I haven't told you this, but I'm going to apply to C. U. just as soon as I get home, and if I'm accepted, keep your fingers crossed, I'll be in Boulder myself before you know it, right along with you. Won't that be great?"

He drew back, frowning. "What makes you think I'll be in Boulder?"

"Because that's where you won the scholarship, isn't it?"

"But that doesn't mean I'll take it."

She stared at him, puzzled. "Why wouldn't you take it? It's a marvelous opportunity, a once-in-a-lifetime chance."

"A chance for what?"

"Why, to have a better life. To escape—" she stopped, biting her lip.

"Escape from this?" he said gruffly, putting out a hand in an all-encompassing gesture. "Is that what you mean, Phoebe?"

She didn't answer, and he went on in a voice of deadly quiet, "Just what's wrong with this, I'd like to know." In the dim light she could see his face was splotched with red, and she realized, too late, that she'd hurt him deeply.

"Oh, Cody, don't get mad." Trying to make amends, she ran

her fingers lightly across his chest and added quickly, "Your home is nice, really sweet. I mean that, but—"

"You wouldn't want to live here. Is that it?"

Honesty compelled her to say, "Well, not forever. I wouldn't mind starting out in a place like this—it would be fun. But eventually I'd like to move on to something better. And you can move on, too, if you get an education. Nothing can stop you. I know how smart you are."

He pulled away from her then and stared at the ceiling. "Not smart enough to read you, I guess. Wynonna was right. She said you were an Eastern snob who looked down your nose at people like us."

Phoebe was so shocked, she was speechless for a moment. She swallowed with difficulty and found her voice finally, but to her dismay her voice broke. "You know that's not true!"

"I don't know anything—except it looks like you've gotten your kicks at my expense. Wynonna warned me about girls like you."

"What's Wynonna got to do with this? She's your sister, and I know you love her, but—"

"She's more'n a sister. She's my best friend." He turned his eyes away, and a tense silence enveloped the room. "You gotta understand," he said finally. "Wynonna and me—well, I can't just toss her aside like an old shoe."

"How would you be tossing her aside if you got an education?"

"By getting one, that's how." Struggling up to a sitting position, he put his head in his hands, and there was a kind of anguish in his voice she had never heard before. "I told you, Wynonna doesn't think much of education. She wasn't good in school, and its already driven a wedge between us, my finishing high with honors. She's always complaining we don't have much to talk about anymore. Heck, if I took that scholarship we might really drift apart."

Phoebe stared at him, dumbfounded. "So you're going to give it up? Sacrifice your whole future so you won't get smarter than your sister? Does that make sense?"

He flushed. "I told you—Wynonna's no dummy."

"I'll say she's not. She's got you wrapped around her little finger."

"Now look here—"

"No, *you* look." Struggling up to a sitting position, too, she bravely faced him. "I know you love your sister, that's admirable, and I'm not trying to put her down. But admit it, Cody—the girl's not very practical. Look at all that talk about going to California, your breaking into the movies. That's a harebrained scheme if I ever heard one."

"So what? If Wynonna wants to give it a try—"

"Do *you* want to give it a try? It's your life."

"You're mistaken. It's *our* life, Wynonna's and mine."

"Oh?" She felt as if his words were pulling the breath out of her body, and a cold knot formed in her stomach. "Sorry. Guess I read this all wrong."

"You read what wrong?"

"This—" She spread out her hands in a gesture taking in the bed, the two of them. "What we felt for each other. I thought it was something wonderful, unique."

"It is unique." Reaching out he put his hands on her shoulders and tried to draw her close again.

But she twisted away. "No!" She felt tears flooding her eyes. But something stronger than tears made her say it. "I think your sister has too much influence on you, Cody, way too much. Maybe that's not for me to decide. But I couldn't share you with Wynonna."

"What? Are you asking me to choose between the two of you?"

"Yes—if that's the way it has to be. I guess what it boils down to is the scholarship and me—if you still want me—and all that implies for a bright future. Or stay with Wynonna and stagnate. It's up to you."

He took a deep breath and closed his eyes, and she could see the struggle going on inside him. Apprehension coursed through her, and as she watched, something dark began rising inside her, starting in the pit of her stomach and spreading out to her fingers, her arms. her head.

Finally he opened his eyes and said simply, "I'm sorry. I don't expect you to understand, but I can't turn my back on my sister. No way."

"Especially not for some fool girl you just met a few days ago, right?"

His silence was all the answer she needed.

In a little while they got up from the bed and dressed, not looking at each other. The pain was like a brick wall between them. They drove back to the lodge in deadly silence. Phoebe knew, glancing at the stubborn mask of his face, that she'd lost him for good, and only her pride kept her from falling apart completely.

Chapter Eleven

*A*s she walked out into the hall the next morning, her whole body was stiff and sore, and dark circles showed beneath her eyes. She felt drained, and a great sadness had settled on her, as though the whole world had turned completely upside down in a single moment. She was filled with confusion, despair. Although she tried to be a good sport and not spoil the trip for her aunt, there was a hollow feeling inside her, the likes of which she had never experienced before.

They stopped in Fairplay for breakfast in one of those Western cafes that looked like it had been lifted straight out of a TV movie. The food was okay, but Phoebe was so miserable, she couldn't eat. Tears kept welling up in her eyes. At first Weezy pretended not to notice.

But after breakfast when it was Phoebe's turn to take the wheel and her driving became erratic—the sun glaring on the macadam made everything waver in the heat, and seeing the road through the prism of her tears was difficult—Weezy said, "Pull over, sweetie. If you want to talk, I'm all ears. But if you don't, just put your head back and rest."

"All right. Thanks." Phoebe was ashamed of her weakness, but her heart was an open wound, and she tortured herself with regrets. Even flunking the audition in New York hadn't hurt as much as losing Cody.

What did I do wrong? she asked herself. *How did it happen? Why?* But there was no answer.

Cody's words of the night before had hit her like a physical blow. In turmoil, she tried to convince herself she'd forget him, although she didn't really believe it. After a while, her mind became numb. She forced herself to stop crying and stoically resumed her share of the driving. They reached Denver before noon and checked in at the motel where Weezy had made a reservation.

"Want to call Jenna for me while I unpack?" Weezy asked, handing Phoebe a slip of paper. "Here's her number. Tell her we'll pick her up around one—if that's convenient for her."

"Okay," Phoebe said. She dialed the number, and a few seconds later she heard her grandmother's high-pitched voice in her ear.

"Sugar baby!" Jenna cried. "Oh, I just can't wait to see you, darling girl!"

Her grandmother had never been what Phoebe would call quiet, and the deafer she became, the louder she talked. And the less she listened.

"Are you still my precious Pavlova?" she went on. "Are those twin brothers of yours as cute as ever? Is your ma still mad enough to kill Franny?"

Phoebe dutifully answered yes to all questions, not that it made any difference. Jenna rattled on enthusiastically as Phoebe held the phone a few inches from her ear, until finally she got a chance to interrupt with the all-important question.

"When are we going to see Franny and the baby, Gram?"

"Right away, of course. I told Franny we'd come over to their place just as soon as you arrived. We're all going out to lunch, even Shilo Dawn."

"Isn't she kind of young for that?"

"Not on your life. Wait'll you see her. Talk about good! That baby's an absolute love. I could eat her up, although I still can't figure out what Franny was thinking of naming that darling child Shilo. If she'd had any sense, she would have named her Phyllis, after your mother, and maybe brought a little peace to the family.

81

Phyllis is a beautiful name, but you can't tell Franny anything. Well, see you soon, honey."

"Yes, soon," Phoebe said, grinning in spite of herself. Hanging up, she turned to Weezy. "My dear grandma!" she exclaimed. "As Dad would say, she sure takes the cake, that lady."

Weezy lifted an eyebrow. "Now what?"

"Oh, she doesn't like Shilo Dawn's name. According to her Franny should have named the baby Phyllis to get on Mom's good side. Can you beat it?"

Weezy smiled. "I don't always agree with my dear sister, but she might have a point. Frankly, I'm a little baffled myself as to why Franny named the baby Shilo Dawn. I know Shiloh, spelled with an *h*, is the name of a famous Civil War battlefield, but what's the connection with the baby, I wonder?"

"No connection," Phoebe said. "Shilo, without the *h*, is also the name of a song by Neil Diamond, who Mom had a crush on at one time. She used to play his tapes all the time when we were growing up. Franny herself was never a big Diamond fan, but she liked the name Shilo. She thought it was quirky, not so run-of-the-mill, you know? As for the Dawn part—"

"Wait. Don't tell me." Weezy put up her hands, her eyes twinkling. "Let me guess. Could it be that the sun was just coming over the horizon when the baby was born, and our Franny took that as a good omen?"

"You've got it." Phoebe nodded, grinning again. "Anyway, you've gotta admit it's better than Phyllis, which Gram is so gung-ho on. Franny and I often wondered why Gram stuck Mom with that moniker. Do you like it, Weezy? Be honest."

"Not especially," Weezy said. "When your mother was born, I thought she ought to be called Joy. Her birth seemed like such a miracle."

"'Cause Gram and Gramps had tried for so long to have a baby, you mean? Gram told us about that one summer when Franny and I were out here visiting."

"Oh? What did she tell you?"

"Why, just that they'd almost given up hope of ever having a baby of their own." She remembered her grandmother saying, "You can't imagine how frustrating it was. Here your grandpa and I had been married for five years and had so much to give a child. We thought so, anyway. But no matter how we tried, nothing happened. Then, when we'd almost resigned ourselves to being childless, didn't I get pregnant our very last year in New York! Our little Phyllis was born in the spring, shortly before the war ended. That meant the three of us could return to Denver, a real family at last."

Phoebe added, "Gram always seemed to think that Mom's birth was a miracle, too. So Joy would have been appropriate."

"Yes. But Jenna had her own ideas," Weezy said. "Although she's probably forgotten about it now, she named the baby after an actress named Phyllis Thaxter, who was popular during World War Two. Thaxter was never a really big star, but she was in this hit movie called *Thirty Seconds Over Tokyo* with Van Johnson, an actor your grandmother adored. She must have seen that movie half a dozen times at least, and I'm sure if the baby had been a boy, she would have insisted on calling the poor child Van."

Weezy's lips trembled for a second, then smiling she gave herself a little shake and added lightly, "But it was *her* baby. She could pick any name she wanted. So, if you're ready, let's get this show on the road. Whatta you say?"

"Fine with me."

They went out to the car, and Weezy pulled out on West Colfax with easy competence and started driving toward Skyview Manor, an assisted-living residence where Jenna had lived since she'd broken her hip two years before. For years she'd had a lovely home in the exclusive Cherry Hills section of Denver, but Phoebe knew from overhearing her parents talk that the beautiful home was mortgaged to the hilt, while Jenna kept on spending like there was no tomorrow. The big house had been sold, and things were supposed to be more or less under control, although, as Phoebe remembered her mom saying, you could never be sure of anything with Jenna.

She was waiting for them in the lobby when they arrived, a

pretty woman with carefully coiffed blond hair atop a rosy pink-cheeked face surprisingly free of wrinkles. Jenna McPherson, at seventy-five and using a walker, was still an attractive woman, Phoebe thought. But it was her grandmother's effervescence that was so beguiling. Although it wore a little thin after a while, it was still wonderfully warm and endearing.

"Weezy! Phoebe!" she cried. "Oh, you adorable things to come all this way to see funny old Jenna." She hugged them both with great gusto, then held them off at arm's length. "Let me look at you! You're both so gorgeous, I can't stand it. How'd I ever get into such a good-looking family?"

Phoebe laughed. "Oh, Gram, you're cute."

"And just as sassy as ever, I see," Weezy said fondly. "Hello, sis. How you feeling?"

"Can't complain," Jenna said. "Course this old thing," she rattled the walker, "tends to put a damper on my charm. Although not completely." She smiled slyly. "See that fella over there?"

Weezy and Phoebe turned in the direction of Jenna's pointing chin and saw a little dried-up prune of a man, balding, with a sparse salt-and-pepper mustache, standing in the doorway of a room down the hall.

"That's Reverend Porter," Jenna informed them. "He's officially retired, but he still practices his profession, or tries to, in here. The other night he came to my room after I was in bed, saying he wanted to save me. Which wouldn't have been such a bad idea, except the dear boy wasn't wearing a thing except his Bible."

"Jenna, you're making that up," Weezy said when she and Phoebe stopped giggling.

"Nope. It's gospel, I swear. This place is full of crazies. But there's never a dull moment."

"What did you say to the preacher, Gram?" Phoebe asked, wiping her eyes.

"Say? Lord, darling. I didn't *say* anything. I just screamed bloody murder until the nurses came and led the poor thing away."

As she talked, the three of them had started walking down

the hall. When they came opposite the preacher, Jenna shook her finger at him playfully. "Hello there, you silly old goat," she said, smiling sweetly. "Deaf as a post," she added, in an aside to Weezy and Phoebe.

The preacher rewarded them all with a beatific smile.

When they got to the car, Jenna said she couldn't wait for them to see the baby. "She's so adorable," she told them. "A perfect little beauty if I ever saw one."

"But what about Franny?" Phoebe asked. "How's Franny doing, Gram?"

Jenna shrugged. "Franny's Franny, you know that, honey. Your big sister will never change. Stubborn as ever—and no one's going to tell her a thing."

"Umm-mm. Do you like this guy she's living with?"

Jenna surprised her by saying, "Yes, very much. Oh, Buck wouldn't win any handsome-guy prizes, but he's sweet and considerate. And he thinks the world of Franny and the baby."

"Then that's all that matters, isn't it?" Phoebe said.

"Not quite," Jenna informed her. "Buck is still just a cook; remember? And not some fancy French chef, either, but just a plain old ordinary hash-slinger in a family restaurant. That's one reason your mother doesn't approve of him, Phoebe. I know my Phyllis."

"I know her, too," Phoebe said. "And I think in spite of her disappointment or disapproval or whatever you want to call it, Mom will come around. Nothing's going to keep her from that baby."

"I hope not," Jenna said. "Still, I suppose we shouldn't be too hard on your mother. After all, when she was growing up girls running off and leaving their husbands wasn't as common as it seems to be today."

"And especially not if said husband is rich and handsome and a doctor," Phoebe added dryly.

Jenna nodded. "My point exactly. Young Malcolm Edgerly had everything going for him and would probably have given Franny a wonderful life. It's a mystery to me why that marriage didn't last. And after that extravagant wedding, the trousseau, the Caribbean honeymoon, that divine apartment that looked straight out of *Architectual Digest.*" Jenna sighed. "No wonder Phyl, and to a lesser extent your dad, too, I suspect, are upset and have washed their hands of Miss Franny. After all, they don't even know Buck Hadley."

Which was her parents' loss, Phoebe decided a little later, when she met Buck for the first time. A burly, muscular young man with a headful of wiry brown curls, she liked him the moment he opened the door. He had warm, friendly brown eyes and a wide, engaging smile that grew even wider when he saw who was standing there.

"You must be Phoebe," he said, taking her hand in both of his and drawing her close to kiss her cheek. "I'd know you anywhere. You look exactly like your pictures. And this pretty lady has to be Aunt Weezy." He kissed her, too. "Franny's told me so much about you both—all good—I feel I already know you. And last but not least, here's Grandma Jenna." He hugged Jenna enthusiastically. "How are you today, gorgeous? Still fighting the guys off with a stick?"

"You'd better believe it," Jenna said and they all laughed.

"So come in, come in." He gestured hospitably, and they went inside the house, one half of a semiattached bungalow in a neighborhood of small homes with one-car garages, across the street from an amusement park Phoebe looked quickly around and couldn't help thinking what a far cry this was from the sleek, modern condo Franny had shared with Mal, which had been a wedding present from Mal's parents.

Yet there was something cozy about this little place. Its sunshine yellow walls and its bright red rug gave it a certain raffish charm. Not much furniture, but lots of bright prints and flowering plants filled the space, and starched white curtains hung at all the windows.

Suddenly a door in back opened and Franny, a striking brunette dressed in jeans and a sweater, strolled in. Barefoot and smiling, Franny had lovely blue eyes, set wide under arched brows, and was so slender Phoebe could hardly believe she'd recently had a baby.

She cried, "Weezy! Phoebe! Oh, it's so good to see you both. And, Gram—how you doing today?"

There followed a lot of hugging and kissing, although all conversation was suspended temporarily due to the roar of the roller-coaster from the amusement park across the way.

"Good heavens, how often does that thing go by?" Phoebe asked, shaken.

"About every fifteen minutes or so." Franny grinned. "Horrendous, isn't it? But believe it or not, you learn to talk around it."

She went into the kitchen then and soon came back with a tray of cheese and crackers, and tall glasses filled with frosty drinks. Then she disappeared again.

But in a few minutes she was back, holding an infant in her arms. "Tah-dah!" she said. "May I present our little princess?"

Both Phoebe and Weezy were struck momentarily speechless at the sight of the baby, who was truly a beautiful child with an all-encompassing smile and delicate features. But it was her coloring that caught and held Phoebe's attention with her vivid green eyes, the riot of bright red curls.

"That hair!" Phoebe said. "Those eyes! Where did they come from?"

Franny shrugged. "Beats me. I told Buck it must be the milkman."

"Except we don't have a milkman." Buck grinned. "We also don't know of any red hair or green eyes in either side of the family. So it's a real mystery where Shilo gets her coloring."

"Perhaps it's a gift from heaven," Weezy said. Then she reached for the baby as if she couldn't wait a second longer, and when Franny relinquished her, Weezy sat down on the sofa, cuddling the little girl close against her breast. "Just look at the darling," she marveled, staring down in loving fascination. "Now I ask you—was there ever anything so perfect?"

She picked up one of the little hands, kissed each tiny finger, then laid her cheek against the soft pink skin. She made soft cooing sounds, and the smiling baby responded in kind. "I love you, precious—oh, how I love you!" she whispered.

She touched the baby's eyes, her cheeks, her lips with gentle fingers as if she could never get enough of this miracle. Watching her, Phoebe got a lump in her throat so big, it almost choked her. She thought of Cody again. She would have liked to have had a baby with Cody someday. But that was impossible now, she thought sadly. Best put it behind her.

"We think she's pretty nice," Franny was saying. "There wasn't a mark on her when she was born. That's because she came so fast. I barely had time to get to the hospital, and I didn't have any labor to speak of. I just gave one big push, and *poof*, there she was. The doctor said I was made to have babies, and I wouldn't mind having a slew."

"Now let's not get carried away," Buck said, but Phoebe noticed how his face lit with pride and adoration when he looked at Franny, and their baby.

Soon Buck left for his job. A little later Franny stuck her feet into a pair of flip-flops, then packed the baby's stuff into what looked like a giant carry-all. It amazed Phoebe how much paraphernalia a little baby seemed to need, just to be taken out the door. But finally everything was ready.

They went to a restaurant on Wadsworth Boulevard, a bright, bustling place where Buck was employed as chef, although he couldn't sit with them since he was too busy in the kitchen. "But I want you to order anything you'd like on the menu, and I'll take care of it," he told them. "It's not every day in the week that I entertain such lovely ladies—and all in the family, too. I'm overwhelmed!"

"Your young man is very nice," Weezy said to Franny when Buck had disappeared into the kitchen.

Franny smiled. "I think so. Not that we could ever convince Mom of that, I'm afraid."

"Give her time," Weezy said, smiling at the baby who lay in her carrier, tucked in the booth between her and Jenna. The little girl kept looking around her, wide-eyed, as if fascinated by what she saw, while contentedly sucking on her pacifier.

"Your mother's just a bit old-fashioned," Jenna reminded Franny.

"Old-fashioned nothing," Franny said. "That lady's straight out of the Dark Ages, if you ask me. Why can't Mom join the twenty-first century and get a little hip, like you two?"

Weezy and Jenna both laughed heartily at that. But, Phoebe realized, Franny was dead serious. She dug into her beef fajitas. The others had opted for fried chicken and barbecued ribs, but Phoebe loved Tex-Mex, and the food was delicious and the portions almost too generous.

"Did Buck really cook all this?" she asked Franny. "It's really good."

Franny looked amused. "Why so surprised, little sister? Buck's an honor graduate of the Culinary Institute in Hyde Park, New York, I'll have you know. He's planning on opening his own restaurant."

"No kidding? When?"

"Soon. Just as soon as he can get his hands on thirty thousand bucks. A friend of ours, who already has his share of the money, is going in with him. They've already found the perfect spot, a deserted warehouse near Evergreen. It needs some repairs, but they plan on doing most of the work themselves. All Buck needs is someone to stake him for the thirty thou, and they'll take off like a house afire."

"But thirty thousand? Golly!" Phoebe whistled softly. "That's a lot of money."

Franny shook her head. "Not really, compared to what they can make. But these bankers out here are just so tight, you wouldn't believe it. They're always turning Buck down, saying he doesn't have any collateral. Have you ever heard of anything so silly? It's not as though he's afraid of hard work, and he's plenty smart. It just makes me so mad I could spit. But I have a hunch that's going to change. I don't know how, but you know what they say—you can't keep a good man down."

Franny's confidence in her baby's father was both touching and impressive, Phoebe thought. Plainly she expected great things of Buck Hadley, which probably explained why she didn't mind living in that tacky little house. Obviously she didn't expect to live there forever, and she must feel that whatever sacrifices she made now would be well worth it. In the long run.

Chapter Twelve

$\mathcal{P}$hoebe was even more sure of her sister's devotion to Buck Hadley the next day when she went alone to visit Franny and the baby, after dropping Weezy off at Jenna's residence. She was a little concerned by a conversation she'd overheard that morning from the motel bathroom, while Weezy was making a call to her bank. It sounded to her like Weezy was going to transfer a considerable amount of money to an account that would help pay for Jenna's continued care in that very expensive assisted-living place she stayed at. Apparently even the sale of Jenna's house had not been enough to cover all her expenses, as Mom and Dad had hoped. But was Weezy in a position to pick up the slack? Phoebe wondered, worried. Could she afford it?

They all planned to meet again at twelve for lunch. In the meantime Phoebe was having a ball helping Franny give Shilo a bath, even if more water ended up on the floor than in the basin.

"Boy, what a fish," she said, trying to hang on to the slippery little body. "Is she always this lively?"

"Always." Franny nodded. "This kid takes after her dad. You might not guess to look at him, but Buck's pretty lively, too. But enough of us. What about you? Are you happy?"

Happy? The question caught her completely off guard, and she could feel her stomach tighten. "Happy enough," she murmured, dropping her eyes.

"Yeah? Well, you sure don't look it," Franny said. "Are you still sad that you didn't make the ballet-school audition? That must have been a real bummer, after all your years of hard work."

"It was. But I've gotten over it."

"Sure?"

"Almost sure," she replied. "I know now I'll never set the ballet world on fire, and one part of me will always regret it. But I can still dance, have a career in dance, if I want it."

"Of course you can," Franny said. "Why do I have the feeling there's something more? What's really bothering you, honey? You can tell me."

Phoebe sighed. She'd never been able to keep anything from her big sister. From the time they were kids, Franny had always been able to see right through her. Apparently nothing had changed.

"Is it a guy?" she was saying now. "Does your love life leave something to be desired?"

"What love life?" Phoebe said.

"Oh, you know. Boyfriends, stuff like that. Do you have a boyfriend?" Franny prompted, gently squeezing water over the baby's head with a sponge.

"Nope," Phoebe said. "But I did meet this really neat guy at the resort where Weezy and I stopped for five days before we got here."

"Sounds interesting. Tell me more," Franny encouraged.

So Phoebe told her hesitantly, stumbling over the words. "I thought we had a lot going for us," she concluded. "We really seemed to be on the same wavelength, you know? But when he told me he was turning down the C. U. scholarship rather than hurt his sister's feelings, I was absolutely flabbergasted. I mean, it was like I didn't know him at all. Suddenly he was this stranger I'd been sleeping with."

"Are you sorry about that?" Franny asked, watching her closely. "The sleeping bit, I mean?"

"No," Phoebe said, remembering how the touch of Cody's lips on her mouth and along her body had driven her wild with desire.

She trembled just thinking about it. Would she ever get over Cody Moon? She thought it highly unlikely. "I'll never be sorry we made love," she confessed, "even if it ended so badly. From the moment I saw Cody, something was different. It was like he was my destiny. Do you think that's dumb of me?"

"Not at all," Franny said. "It happens that way sometimes. *Un coup de foudre*, the French call it, falling in love at first sight. Seeing someone and knowing beyond a shadow of a doubt that he's the one for you."

"Exactly." Phoebe nodded. "Meeting Cody was the most wonderful, the most thrilling experience of my life." And that was the truth, she thought sadly. She remembered everything about him, the sweet smile, the deep blue eyes, the sun-colored hair, the way he held her in his arms when he kissed her. The feel of his fingers against her skin, the sound of his voice in her ear when he said how much he loved her—it made her heart ache just thinking about it.

When she spoke again, her voice was almost a whisper. "I love him, I really do, Franny. And I thought he loved me, too. I was sure of it really. But I blew it, fool that I am. I read him all wrong. How could I have been so stupid?"

"Don't be so hard on yourself," Franny told her. "Remember how long I went with Mal? I was pinned to him all through college. We were officially engaged for more than a year. And in all that time, if anyone had asked me, I would have said we had the perfect relationship."

"Well, you seemed to," Phoebe agreed. "When you brought him home for visits, Mom always said Mal had you right up there on a pedestal."

"He did. Absolutely. He was the most incredible guy, and about the only male I ever went with who never tried to get into my panties. He thought so highly of me, respected me so much, he said he didn't even want to have sex until I was his wife."

"Did you like that?"

"What do you think?" Franny grinned wryly. "I hated it, to be honest, but I went along with it. Mal was studying so hard to get into med school, spending so much time on the books, I convinced myself it would probably be better if we didn't get involved that way until we were married. But we did a lot of necking, pretty heavy stuff, too, and when Mal drew back, I admired him for having so much control."

She brushed a strand of hair from her eyes and continued, "Then he graduated, made med school, finally became an M. D. When he began his internship and we were married, I thought all my dreams were coming true at last." She stopped suddenly, and a long silence followed.

"So what happened?" Phoebe remembered a picture Franny had sent the family of her and Mal on their honeymoon. It had been taken by a hotel pool, with the blue waters of the Caribbean behind them. Mal was sitting in a deck chair, a happy smile on his clean-cut, all-American face, and a radiant Franny stood behind him. She was leaning over him, her arms around his neck, her chin resting lightly on his head. He had grasped her wrists with both hands, and they looked, for all the world, like an advertisement for young couple in love.

"Was Mal—mean in some way?" she prompted, although she couldn't imagine such a thing.

"No, never!" Franny shook her head emphatically. "We never had a cross word. I loved him, and he loved me. But" —she ran a hand across her eyes — "he was working such horrendous hours at the hospital, I hardly saw him for days on end. He worried about me spending so much time alone, and he encouraged me to go out with my girlfriends and visit the folks. Remember that last visit I made home a few months after we were married?"

Phoebe nodded. "Vaguely. As I recall you didn't stay very long."

"No, I cut the visit short. I missed Mal so much, I couldn't stay away, even though he was so busy I didn't see much of him. When he did get home," she continued, "he was so exhausted, he fell asleep as soon as his head hit the pillow. But a little bit of Mal was better than nothing. I actually ached to feel his arms around me."

So, as she reminded Phoebe, she changed her ticket, over their mother's objections, and caught an early flight back to Denver. The plane got in at eight, and she took a taxi to the apartment. She unlocked the door and let herself in very quietly. The hall was dark, but she saw a faint light coming from under the bedroom door. She wondered if Mal had fallen asleep with the light on and smiled, imagining the joy on his face when he saw her.

She opened the bedroom door, crying gaily, "Darling, I'm home!" Then she glanced at the bed where her young husband was lying, and froze. Mal, naked, was locked in a passionate embrace with another man! At the sound of her voice, he yanked his lips from his lover's and, turning, saw her standing there. As long as she lived she would never forget the stricken look in his eyes. Or how his face seemed to shatter into a million little pieces.

"Franny," he said brokenly. "What are you doing here? I didn't expect you."

"That's obvious."

"Why didn't you call?"

"I wanted to surprise you."

"Well, you sure did—surprise me, I mean." His lips curved in a feeble attempt at a smile and he made an even more feeble attempt to cover his nakedness. But the other man, hogging the sheet, had scooted down in the bed, and Mal was left exposed.

She felt sick, she told Phoebe, like she might throw up. A cold sweat broke out all over her and she shivered from head to foot. It was so unexpected, so jolting, she was in a state of shock. Turning blindly away, she stumbled to the kitchen and sat down at the table, hugging herself. "Oh, my God! My God!" she whispered brokenly.

She was dazed, appalled at what she'd just seen, and at the same time filled with utter disbelief. That couldn't have been Mal, not *her* Mal, making love with another man. It would have broken her heart if she'd found him with a woman—but this was worse, a thousand times worse!

She didn't know how long she sat there, her mind in a turmoil, her eyes unseeing except for that hideous picture in the bedroom, which kept playing over and over in her head. After a while she heard murmurings from the bedroom, and the front door open and close. She assumed the other man had dressed and left. A short time later Mal, wearing his terrycloth robe, came into the kitchen and sat down across from her.

"We have to talk." He put out one finger, tentatively, but she drew away.

"Don't touch me.!"

"I'm so sorry, darling."

"Don't darling me. You—you've betrayed me!"

"I know—I've betrayed myself. I'd give anything if you hadn't seen. But I want you to know what happened, back there in the bedroom, has nothing to do with us."

"Liar! Are you insane?" She was screaming at him now. "You must be insane! Why did you marry me?"

"Because I want a normal life. I want a wife, children, the kind of home I grew up in. I still want that."

"Yeah? You have a funny way of showing it, mister. That—that man," she could hardly get the words out. "Who is he?"

Mal shrugged. "Just someone from the hospital who helped me with a patient. I offered him a ride home and, because it was early, asked him in for a drink. We had two or three drinks. I can't remember, I was so tired. I haven't had any sleep in about eighteen hours, and somehow we ended up in bed."

"Have you done this before?"

"No, never." His brows drew together in an agonized expression, then he dropped his eyes. "Well, hardly ever," he admitted, after a moment. "There were a few times in med school, but it didn't mean anything—and it'll never happen again. I swear it! If you could just find it in your heart to forgive me—please! Will you forgive me?"

Her heart was hammering, her breathing ragged, her chest felt as if it would burst. But he looked so broken, so pathetic, she could feel herself weakening in spite of herself. "Oh, Mal, I don't know...."

He quickly took her up on it. "I'll spend the rest of my life trying to make it up to you, I promise. I don't want to lose you, Franny, darling. I love you. Don't you love me still—just a little?"

"Yes," she confessed. Of course she did. He had hurt her terribly and her heart felt as if it had been torn in half, but she still loved him, wanted him...

"Then let's try to forget it," Mal said. "We'll put it behind us like a bad dream. It has nothing to do with our life together, sweetheart."

She was still so shaken, so upset, she couldn't think straight. But she wanted desperately to believe him. So she convinced herself he was tired, he'd had too much to drink; it was the other man's fault. The other man looked older in that one fleeting glimpse she'd had of him, before he'd hidden his head in the covers. He'd probably seduced Mal—poor Mal. She shouldn't have left him, shouldn't have exposed him to temptation.

"I couldn't live without you," he was saying. "I'm only half-alive when you're not around. Oh, Franny, Franny precious, I'm so sorry, so ashamed." He looked at her beseechingly, his eyes filled with tears, and when he reached for her this time she didn't draw away.

Somehow her arms went around him, comforting him. Then he was kissing her as if he could never get enough of her lips. They ended up making love on the sofa. He wanted to take her to bed, but she couldn't go to that bed, those sheets, at least not yet, remembering what had gone on there just a short time before. And Mal understood.

In the next few months he did everything he could to make her happy, and their marriage was stronger than it had ever been. He spent all his time with her when he wasn't at the hospital, and even when he was there he called her two or three times a day just to say he loved her. So she forgot what she'd seen that night in the bedroom. It was an aberration, she told herself, that would never happen again. And she really believed that.

At Christmas Mal got five days off unexpectedly, and they went to Aspen skiing, returning to Denver on New Year's Eve just in time for the chief resident's party. They were both tired after all that sunshine and exercise and would have much preferred staying home. But Mal said, "We probably should put in an appearance, at least. The guy is the chief resident after all, and I hear he keeps track of things like that. Would you mind going terribly, darling?"

"Of course not," Franny said, good sport that she was. She put her arms around him and hugged him and thought how lucky she was to have a handsome young husband who adored her. So they went to the party and, all in all, had a pretty good time.

No matter where she went in the room, she felt Mal's eyes upon her. At midnight they exchanged kisses, and she felt a tingle of excitement thinking of what was to come later. Mal was obviously thinking along the same lines.

"I have this incredible urge to tear off that pretty dress you're wearing," he whispered in her ear, "and throw you down on the floor and—"

"Shh-hh. Control yourself, boy." Laughing, she reached up and put her fingers across his lips. "Our time will come soon enough. But now we ought to mingle with the other guests, make a good impression. Don't you think?"

"If you promise not to stray too far. Remember who you came with, *Mrs.* Edgerly."

"As if I could forget." She laughed. But the next time someone asked her to dance she accepted.

She danced with all of Mal's colleagues and had several glasses of champagne, and eventually had to pee. But the bathroom door was locked, and there was only one bathroom in the apartment. Chief resident or not, this place wasn't half as nice as hers and Mal's apartment, she thought a trifle smugly.

Ten minutes later she tried the bathroom door again, but it was still occupied. "Gosh, I wonder what's going on in there?" she said.

"Wouldn't have a guess." A young woman standing in front of the bedroom mirror, combing her long chestnut hair, shrugged. "But if you're desperate, there's a lav in the laundry room. It's out that door," she pointed, "at the end of the corridor. I know because we live upstairs and there's a laundry room on each floor."

"Why, thanks. I'll try that," Franny said. She went out into the hall and walked down the corridor. She found the laundry room without any trouble. The light was off, but she could see several washers and dryers in the light from the corridor; she also saw a side door marked Restroom.

Quickly she walked over to that door and opened it. The light was on and she was startled to see two men inside. One was sitting on the toilet seat holding the other man astride his lap. They had their arms around each other and were oblivious to anything else as they kissed.

She wasn't aware that she'd made a sound but unconsciously she must have gasped, and the two abruptly pulled apart. They turned and looked up at her and she saw the arrogant, young-old face of the chief resident. The other man, sitting on his lap, was Mal.

"A part of me died that night," Franny told Phoebe as they bathed the baby. "Even now, when I think of it, it aches. But I've gotten over it." She ran a hand across her eyes and smiled bravely. "I had to, or go out of my mind."

"I can't believe it," Phoebe said stunned. "You mean Mal is— gay? Is that what you're saying?"

"That's what I'm saying, little sis. He loved me after a fashion, but he could do it both ways—and he liked it with men better. Much better."

"That—that's incredible!"

"Oh, don't look so shocked. It could be worse. At least Mal's not HIV positive. He didn't give me AIDS."

"Thank God for that. But being gay is still pretty reprehensible in Mom's book."

Franny sighed. "Don't I know. To Mal's folks too, I'm afraid. That's why I haven't told anyone."

"But everyone thinks you just walked out on him, Franny. Everyone blames you for the break-up of your marriage."

"So what? I don't mind playing the heavy." Franny's pretty

mouth, sweetly bowed and generous, curved in a smile. "Mal's still got a year of residency to complete. There could be some bigots on the hospital board. Why ruin it for him? When he's ready he'll come out. In spite of all the lies he told me he's basically an honest person, a decent man. And now that the shock's gone, believe it or not we're still friends."

"Oh, Franny, you're really something." Phoebe was so choked up she couldn't say any more. But she'd never been so proud of her sister.

She watched as Franny lifted the squirming baby from the water and placed her on the changing table. Lovingly she dried her and buried her face in the baby's stomach, making gurgling sounds until Shilo was convulsed with giggles.

"Anyway, it doesn't matter anymore," Franny was saying. "I'm happy now, even if the money is kind of tight. Buck's a wonderful guy. And,"—she blushed "—he can't keep his hands off me." Lifting her head she added, almost shyly, "So, tell the truth now, do you like him?"

"Yes," Phoebe said without a moment's hesitation. "A lot. I know Mom and Dad would like him, too, if—"

"If we got hitched? Well, relax, it's coming. Buck and I are going to get married, probably in the fall. He wanted to get married before the baby came, but I wasn't in any hurry. Our getting married isn't going to change anything. Buck is already my husband for all practical purposes. He's going places, you'll see. He's plenty ambitious, and he wants to give Shilo all the advantages we had."

She pulled a little shirt over the baby's head. "Of course I can help, too, and I intend to. As soon as Shilo's a little older, we'll find a good daycare center and I'll go back to work. After all I didn't get my degree for nothing, and I want to use it."

"Good for you. I know you and Buck will make a go of it, Franny."

"Sure, we will. There're no flies on us guys; huh, Shilo?" She bussed the baby again, bringing on another fit of giggles. Then turning to Phoebe she added, "I just wish something nice would happen to you."

"Thanks. Me, too," Phoebe said, blinking. But she didn't count on it; she knew that would just be wishful thinking.

Chapter Thirteen

$\mathcal{A}$s they got ready for bed that night, after telling her the whole story, Phoebe said to Weezy, "Franny thinks Mal really wanted to change. He tried—but the other thing was just too strong, I guess. She feels he couldn't help himself."

"That's probably true." Weezy nodded. "I can't imagine anyone choosing that lifestyle deliberately, with all the prejudice people like that have to put up with. I believe a person's born that way."

"So does Franny. But it was still a terrible blow when she found out."

"I can imagine." Weezy sighed. "No wonder the poor child sounded so sad around that time."

"Yeah, but she's not sad any longer. She loves Buck, and they'll do all right. Maybe they're kind of broke right now, but he's going to open his own restaurant, just as soon as he can get his hands on thirty thousand bucks. And they plan on getting married in the fall. I hope that changes things with Mom. She's so set in her ways."

"That's her nature, honey. But you mustn't be too hard on your mother. After all, in her day, most so-called nice girls didn't have babies out of wedlock. There was a certain stigma attached to it."

"Maybe then, but nobody thinks anything of it now. Just look at all the movie stars who have babies today, with no husband in the picture. Anyway, you and Gram don't seem to mind about Franny, and you're both a lot older than Mom. Wasn't unwed motherhood frowned on in your day?"

"Frowned on?" Weezy smiled. "That hardly describes it. If a girl had a child out of wedlock in my day she was 'ruint', as the saying goes. That attitude lasted for quite a while, too. After World War Two a famous Hollywood star named Ingrid Bergman had a baby by a man she wasn't married to, and she almost lost her career."

"Why, I know her," Phoebe said. "I've watched Ingrid Bergman lots of times in those old movies on TV. Gosh, was she ever beautiful!"

"She was—and not only that, the American people were so enchanted with her, they'd elevated her almost to sainthood. She was right up there with Joan of Arc. Then she committed this terrible indiscretion, and overnight all her adoring fans turned against her, almost crucified her. Our own senator Johnson from Colorado got up in the Senate and denounced her. The good senator said the public should boycott her films and she shouldn't be allowed to set foot in America again."

"Just because she had a kid by a man she wasn't married to?"

Weezy nodded. "That was the climate in those days. And not only the woman suffered. The baby was called a bastard. Who'd want to saddle an innocent child with a label like that?"

"Not many, I imagine. God!" Phoebe shuddered. "I'm glad Franny wasn't living then."

"Exactly. But that was a long time ago. In the space of two generations, things have taken a one eighty degree turn, and I'm glad. I'm sure your grandma is glad, too. And your mother will come around eventually."

"I hope so," Phoebe said. "But speaking of Gram, didn't you think she acted kind of bitchy today?"

"Bitchy?" Weezy lifted an eyebrow. "I didn't notice."

"Ah, come on. You know what I mean," Phoebe said.

They had all gone out to lunch at an upscale restaurant Grandma Jenna had suggested, but when Weezy picked up the check, Jenna had almost made a scene. "Saints alive!" she had exclaimed, her still attractive face suddenly an unattractive red. "Whoever thought the day would come when Jenna would be taking handouts, letting her once poor-as-a-church-mouse baby sister pay for *everything*. Well, that says something about the merits of the single life, I guess."

To her credit Weezy had refused to take the bait. "I think most likely it says something about trying to reciprocate," she had remarked mildly. "After all, considering all you and Wes did for me when I needed it, Sis, I guess I can pick up a check once in a while."

"These days it's more than once in a while," Jenna had snapped, and she'd pouted for the rest of the afternoon, although she'd perked up a little by the time they arrived at Franny's that evening.

Buck had prepared dinner for them in the cramped kitchen, Cajun shrimp and red rice, and a delectable chocolate mousse for dessert. Everything was delicious, and after a few glasses of wine, Jenna was once more her usual bubbly self. But Phoebe was still puzzled by her grandmother's outburst at lunch.

"If you ask me," she told Weezy, as they got into their pajamas, "Gram was not only kind of bitchy today, but she sounded —well, envious. Which is pretty silly, when you think about it."

Weezy smiled. "Oh, I don't know. People are envious for all kinds of reasons. I remember one rainy day when Mickey and I were having lunch with his friend Rudy Diels—" She paused. "Have I mentioned Rudy to you?"

Phoebe nodded. "Wasn't he the guy who talked Mickey into that crap game, which he won?"

"You've got it," Weezy said. "Rudy was a short, wiry fellow, not at all good looking but lots of fun. He was in Mickey's class at NYU, both of them in Intelligence. He seemed to have a font of information at his fingertips, and he liked nothing better than showing it off. So on this particular day, as we were finishing lunch, I casually remarked that I envied them going to Europe, even if they weren't going under the best of circumstances. And suddenly Rudy jumped to his feet and said not to worry. He said he knew of a place that was just like Europe, right there in New York."

"Oh, sure," Mickey scoffed. "And I remember how he laughed," Weezy said. "Then he asked Rudy if he was going to take us to Little Italy, some new Italian restaurant, maybe, famous for their cannolis? Who's in the mood for dessert?"

Weezy's eyes twinkled, as she related the story. "Never you mind," Rudy said. "He could prove it. So we got on the subway, and after a very long ride, we came out of the train to find the rain had stopped. It was one of the most beautiful fall days I'd ever seen. It was early October and the leaves had started to turn bright reds and oranges and yellows. As we walked along, I could see the high cliffs of the Palisades in the distance, and what looked like the walls of a castle rising up before us. It was hard to believe we were still in Manhattan."

"So what was it?" Phoebe asked, enthralled.

"The place was called the Cloisters," Weezy told her, "and it even had a moat like a real castle. At the entrance we were lucky enough to find a tour just beginning. The guide informed us that the Cloisters was part of the Metropolitan Museum of Art and had been constructed from old buildings that had been brought over, piece by piece, from the Continent.

"The guide gave a fascinating talk about the medieval life of the monks, who had once lived in those buildings, and took us to the room where the famous unicorn tapestries were kept. I remember I shuddered at the tapestry showing the little unicorn being stabbed by hunters. Mickey's and my favorite was the one showing the unicorn lying down in a little fenced-in yard among the flowers. 'Do you know what's that supposed to represent?' Mickey whispered to me. 'Paradise, no less.' "

" 'Oh, listen to the old romantic,' " Rudy, who had heard him, teased. "But Mickey just smiled," Weezy said.

"Then he put his arm around me and asked me the all-important question. 'Will you make me a promise? Please promise you won't marry anyone but me—ever!' "

"What did you say?" Phoebe wanted to know.

"I promised," she said. "And that was the easiest promise I ever made. But to get back to the envy thing, it's ridiculous, but as I said people can envy other people for all kinds of things. So don't be too hard on your grandma, darling. We all have our little quirks, and you must remember it's difficult for Jenna, finding herself in reduced circumstances."

"I guess," Phoebe said. "But most of it she brought on herself, didn't she?"

"Ah, sweetie, you don't know...."

"Sure, I do," Phoebe said. "Lord knows I've heard Mom and Dad talk about it enough. They always said Gram never had any sense when it came to money."

"She didn't have to have much sense when Wes was alive. He took care of everything. And Jenna was always very generous, maybe too generous. So it's hard for her, being on the receiving end now."

"Has she always hated taking things from you?"

"Not always." Weezy shrugged "Once, she wasn't so sensitive about things like that. But now when I try to give her something, it makes her feel sad—and diminished."

"Still, I'd think she'd be a little grateful," Phoebe said. "I heard you talking to your bank this morning, and I suppose it's none of my business, but I know you're helping to pay her way in that nice place where she lives."

"It's the least I can do. Your parents have you and the twins to educate, and certainly Franny and Buck aren't in a position to help. Besides, I have more than I'll ever need."

"Really? That's super. Did you get all that money from—?" she stopped, catching herself just in time. "Sorry." She blushed. "Forget I said that."

She was mortified at her indiscretion, but Weezy laughed. "Nonsense, I know what you're thinking. Did I get my money from my boss, Len Bernard, as your dear mother has always assumed? Well, the answer is yes and no. I never took a cent from him personally. I always paid my own way, and he never tried to force money on me. But he insisted on buying me things, stocks mostly. Every Christmas and birthday, every anniversary and special occasion in all those years, he added blue-chip stocks to my portfolio. I didn't think much about it at the time, since I always lived on my salary and reinvested the dividends. But through the years, without any effort on my part, I became a comparatively wealthy woman."

"No kidding? Gee, that's great. But speaking of Mr. Bernard, you want to hear something funny? When Franny and I used to visit you in the summer, at the cabin in Evergreen, and Mr. Bernard was around, we'd always make bets about whether you two were ever going to get married."

Weezy smiled a bittersweet smile. "People always wondered that. It was only natural, I guess."

"I guess," Phoebe agreed. She remembered Len Bernard as an attractive, robust man in his early sixties when she and Franny met him. He wore his hair in a crew cut and had a warm, friendly face. Both girls had liked him tremendously. And they'd adored Weezy's rustic cabin, tucked into the side of a hill, with a whole glass wall giving a magnificent view of Mount Evans. Often when Franny and Phoebe came to stay at the cabin, Mr. Bernard would be staying at a motel in the nearby village.

"I'll always remember how Mr. Bernard used to take us horseback riding," Phoebe said, "even though the horses made his allergies kick up. Gosh, he was such a nice guy. And he was crazy about you, Weezy. Even a kid could see that."

"Perhaps, but there were complications."

"Oh, I know. Mom told us he had a wife. But he didn't live with her; did he?"

"No. Len's wife was in a private sanatorium in New Jersey. She remained there for over forty-five years."

"Forty-five years?" Phoebe was shocked.

"Alissa, that was his wife's name, was injured in a car accident when she was only twenty-five. It left her in a vegetative state. The doctors said she'd never get any better."

"How awful!" Phoebe said.

"Yes." Biting her lip, Weezy looked away. "Len and I were both on intimate terms with misfortune. I think it brought us closer together."

"Oh?" Phoebe said. Then curious added, "How did you meet Mr. Bernard?"

"I met him through Wes, your grandfather," Weezy told her. "The war had ended, and Jenna and Wes were returning to Denver with their new baby, and I was sort of at loose ends. I'd left Julliard and I needed to find a job and make some money. That's when Wes thought of Len. They'd known each other in college.

"I hear he's starting a little company," Wes had said. "Something to do with finance," he added, which didn't surprise him. He said this Len was a whiz at math.

"I remember a game we used to play in school," Wes said. "Len would ask me to think up a list of numbers, say seventy or a hundred, the bigger the better, and write the numbers down on a slip of paper. Then using a pen or pencil, he'd have me total the numbers, while he added them up in his head. And," Wes laughed, "I didn't consider myself a slouch exactly, but no matter how hard I tried, Len always beat me. He was quite a guy."

"Really? He sounds intimidating to me," Weezy said. "I don't know if I could measure up to someone like that."

" Of course you could," Wes assured her. "You're good at figures. After all, you always straighten out Jenna's checkbook when I'm not around, and that alone"—he laughed again—"qualifies you as an expert, in my opinion. So why don't I give Len a ring? Who knows? You might have a good future together."

And without further ado he arranged a meeting.

Chapter Fourteen

She didn't know what to expect, she told Phoebe, but Len had a Wall Street address and she figured he'd have a pretty nice office. So she was surprised when she got off the elevator in one of the Art Deco buildings in New York's bustling financial district and walked down a corridor and knocked.

"Come in," a voice said, and she opened the door and found herself in a small, spare room. There was a desk, a couple of chairs, metal shelves along one wall crowded with books and folders of various shapes and sizes, and not much else. A young man with a pleasant, open face was sitting behind the desk, talking on the phone. He looked up when she entered the room and smiling, gestured for her to take a seat. Then he went on with his conversation.

"Okay, okay," he said to someone she later learned was his broker. "I know it's a bit chancy. But I've studied the market, and this company has pizzazz, I tell you. So I want you to put me down for five hundred. I'll come up with the cash somehow, don't worry." Still smiling he hung up and turned his attention to Weezy.

"So you're Wes's sister-in-law," he said in a friendly way. "Well, he was right about one thing—you are easy on the eyes. But do you know anything about business?"

"No." Weezy shook her head. "But I can type and answer the phone, and I'm a pretty fast learner. You wouldn't be sorry if you hired me, Mr. Bernard."

He laughed then, and his blue eyes sparkled. "It's Len, and I like your honesty," he told her. "So whatta you say we take a chance and join forces?"

"Fine with me," Weezy said.

He could pay her only twenty-five dollars a week, but she didn't need much. Wes and Jenna had bought the apartment, which she later bought from them, and they were letting her live there rent free for the time being. The only other job she'd been offered was in the lingerie department at Macy's, which paid even less and didn't appeal to her much. She decided to throw in her lot with this dynamic young man who exuded confidence.

And that was the beginning of a relationship that brought her not only a lifestyle far beyond her expectations but more important, a cherished and lasting friendship.

Len Bernard was daring —the initial investment she'd overheard him confirm of five hundred bucks made a tidy profit of ten thousand a few months later. Her confidence in his acumen continued to grow.

But she soon realized there was much more to her new boss than just business smarts. He had an abundance of warmth and patience in his dealings with her that was hard to resist, but he never tried to push things, which would have frightened her off. He confided in her about his wife and how devastated he'd been when the doctors said she'd never get any better, and she found herself sharing her own feelings and fears for Mickey. It brought them closer, and from the beginning he treated her more like a trusted confidante than a lowly employee.

The stock market both challenged and intrigued him, and he passed this fascination on to her with his unbounded energy and enthusiasm. He was ambitious and conducted his business aggressively with a gambler's bent for risk-taking. But he did nothing halfway. Before he invested in a company, he studied it carefully, and nine times out of ten this foresight paid off.

Weezy was impressed, and soon, in addition to typing and answering the phone, she began asking him questions about the market. He found her to be an apt and clever pupil. He admired her shrewdness and insight when it came to his fledgling company, and he knew she shared his concern for their investors.

"These folks are looking to us to protect their capital," he explained, "and they want to see positive returns in both good and bad markets. *Comprendre?*"

"You bet," she said with a grin.

He asked her to tag along the next time he went out of town to check on a company, and for quite a while everything was strictly business. Until one night in Dayton, Ohio, when the motel where they were staying got their reservations botched up and gave them one room, instead of the two adjoining rooms they'd requested. When they checked in the desk clerk was most apologetic, but there was a big VFW convention in town he explained, and hence no extra rooms to be found.

"Oh, dear." Weezy sighed, after the clerk had called half-a-dozen places for them to no avail. "What'll we do?"

"Not to worry," Len said. "I'll bunk on the floor. I've done it lots of times—in camp, in the Army."

And true to his word he got sheets and blankets and a couple of pillows from the housekeeper, while Weezy undressed in the bathroom. When she came back in the room a short time later Len was in his pajamas, stretched out on the floor. "Good-night," he said cheerfully when she turned out the bedside lamp.

"Good-night, Len. Sleep tight," Weezy said, and she hoped very much that would be the case.

But she could hear him tossing and turning as the night wore on. Finally she pushed herself up on one elbow and stared down at him concerned. "What's wrong?" she asked. "Can't you get comfortable?"

"Well, it's a struggle," he admitted. "This old floor's pretty darn hard."

"I was afraid of that," she said. Then deciding, what the heck? she swallowed and added boldly, "You know this is a pretty big bed and I don't take up much room. So if you want to share it, look—it's okay with me."

"You mean it? Now that's an offer I can't refuse." He laughed. He jumped up from the floor, got in bed beside her, and leaning closer kissed her. It was a light feathery kiss that didn't make any demands but suggested delights worth looking into. So that was the start of it.

All in all she had no regrets. He wasn't Mickey, but he was interesting and fun, and they had a good time together. He was appreciative of her hard work and suggestions, and he let her know it.

"You're smart," he told her one night. "You're resourceful and the best-looking girl I know. But the craziest, too—to hook up with a pauper like me."

"But you're not going to stay a pauper." She meant it. She never doubted that he was going to be wildly successful.

And he was! It wasn't long before he was being touted as one of the shrewdest and most successful young venture capitalists on Wall Street, putting together huge real-estate deals and consolidating many businesses and corporate mergers. But through it all he kept his cool. Even later, when he became a hedge-fund manager and made millions betting against mortgage-based securities early on, before housing values plummeted, he took it all in stride and remained modest.

He was kind and unassuming, and more or less accepting of his lot in life—except when it came to Weezy. He hadn't meant for it to happen, but he'd fallen in love, and after awhile he wanted something more permanent.

"Why don't you move your stuff over here?" he said one Sunday as they sat on his sofa, reading the Times. "I've got all this space I'm rattling around in,"—he put out his arms encompassing the new luxury apartment he'd just moved into "—and I'd like nothing better, honey, than sharing it with you."

"Thanks," Weezy said, "but I like my own place." She never moved in with him, although they spent many nights and weekends together. It was a satisfying arrangement for her, and she would have said they were happy, but her reluctance to share his life fully became a bone of contention between them.

"Whatta you say we make some changes?" he said another morning as they lay in bed. "Face it, darling—the war's long gone, your Mickey's not coming back, and my Alissa is never going to get better. I'll see to it that she's well taken care of for the rest of her life, but I don't think anyone would blame me if I got a divorce; do you?"

"No. I'm sure they wouldn't," Weezy said, dreading what she knew was coming next.

"Then let's get married," he coaxed, and bending over he took her face in his hands and held it very gently. "Will you do me the honor of marrying me, sweetheart?"

"Oh, Len, I don't know," she said, turning her head aside. "What's wrong with what we have here?"

"Nothing's wrong with it, but I want more."

And I haven't got any more to give, she thought sadly, torn by conflicting emotions. She knew Len loved her, and she appreciated his desire to make their union permanent, while at the same time telling herself she was nuts not to take him up on his proposal. But marrying him, marrying anybody except the one she was betrothed to in her heart—? She knew her feelings on that score were ridiculous, but she just couldn't help herself. So she jumped up from the bed and started making blueberry pancakes, his favorite, hoping that would be the end of it. And he did let it drop for a while.

But every now and then through the years he'd bring it up, and she often wondered why he had to agonize over it, since she'd told him time and again that she couldn't marry him. Things finally came to a head one night in London.

They had gone there partly for business and partly for pleasure and were staying at the elegant Connaught Hotel in exclusive Mayfair. London was one of Weezy's favorite cities, and while Len looked up an old friend, she spent the day doing all the things she liked best. She had a delicious lunch at The Ivy, in the theater district, which was supposed to be the best place in town for spotting stars. She didn't think she saw any stars that day but she enjoyed the cozy surroundings and thought the clientele looked interesting. Later she did a little shopping in world-famous Harrod's and watched the changing of the guard at Buckingham Palace, which she'd seen many times before but always enjoyed, and ended up, as always, in Piccadilly Circus, which for her was the cherry on the sundae.

She walked around admiring the Memorial Fountain with its statue of Eros, the god of love, and stopped in several of the little curiosity shops. She knew she'd never find the shop where Mickey had bought her the pillbox with its cloisoneé top showing the little unicorn lying in the flowers. That shop probably no longer existed, she told herself, but it didn't matter. As she walked along, fingering the pillbox, which she always carried with her and had taken from her bag. as often happened she felt his presence near her. She wasn't bubbling with joy or anything like that, but feeling his nearness brought her a strange kind of comfort. When she got back to the hotel, she wasn't in any mood to be badgered by Len, but in his nice way, he did seem to be doing just that as he told her about the visit with his friend Jerry.

"Old Jers was the biggest cut-up I ever knew," he said fondly, "but he's happily married now and has three wonderful kids he adores."

"Great," Weezy said.

"He asked me what was holding me back. So I told him I was more than willing, but my lady wouldn't cooperate."

"Oh, Len, please—"

"Please what?" he said. And he came over beside her then and put his hands on her shoulders and shook her slightly. "Don't you think I'm entitled to a little happiness in the years I've got left? You know how much I love you."

"And I love you," Weezy told him. "I consider you a very dear friend and a wonderful companion. Our relationship has always been very special to me."

"Swell. But I don't want a friend or a companion," Len said

wryly. "I want a *wife*. Can't you understand that? I want to see you sitting across from me at dinner every night. I want to wake up and feel you beside me every morning." Suddenly his voice broke, and letting go of her he turned away and walked over to the bank of windows on the opposite wall and stared somberly out the glass. "Not that I don't love our time together," he added when he got control of his voice again. "I love sleeping with you, when you can work me in. But dammit, maybe I'm selfish, but I want *more* than that."

"I know you do, and I'm terribly sorry," Weezy said. "But I can't give you what you want, Len dear. I don't quite understand why myself, but it's just the way it is." She ached with an inner confusion and felt the old pain squeezing her heart when she thought of Mickey, while at the same time she was wracked with guilt over what she was denying this splendid example of a man.

"Look," she said, "if you want to call it quits, I'll understand."

"Oh, for God's sake, don't be ridiculous!" he cried. And turning he sprinted back to her and took her in his arms and squeezed her in a great bear hug. And he said, his voice coming out all muffled and wobbly, "What we have is better than nothing, I guess. And I'm still hoping, fool that I am, that someday I'll get you to change your mind."

Don't count on it, she thought, smiling at him through her tears.

Chapter Fifteen

"So what became of Len?" Phoebe asked that night. "He sounds like such a sweet man."

"That he was." Weezy smiled. "Top-notch in every way. He suffered a cerebral hemorrhage in his sleep and died without gaining consciousness, a while back. It wasn't a bad way to go, considering."

"I guess not," Phoebe said. "But his fortune—what happened to all that money you said he made?" She knew it was really none of her business, but she was curious, and Weezy didn't seem to mind.

"Oh, it all went to a foundation set up in his wife's name. Len and I talked it over several years before he passed on. He knew I didn't need any more money—I had more than enough for a comfortable life—and he could help so many, many people through a foundation. I'm on the board there."

"Yeah? Why that's stupendous, really great," Phoebe said, and she meant it. "But poor Len never succeeded in getting you to marry him?"

"Nope." Weezy shook her head. "I think my reluctance had something to do with not knowing what happened to Mickey. I feared he'd fallen into Colonel Schatgstaff's hands."

"That German SS officer you have nightmares about sometimes?" Phoebe asked.

"Exactly," Weezy nodded. "The SS did terrible things to their captives." She suddenly began to shake, and Phoebe could see she was struggling to control herself.

"We don't have to talk about it if you'd rather not," she said.

"No, it's all right," Weezy assured her, after a moment. "It's just from what I learned later Colonel Schatgstaff was the worst of the worst, and I just couldn't bear to think of someone I loved in his clutches."

"And you think Mickey had been captured by the SS?" Phoebe asked, suddenly realizing she had been holding her breath.

Weezy sighed. "I don't know for sure. That's the trouble. Before then I sensed that Mickey's time at NYU was coming to an end and he'd be leaving for overseas soon, and just the thought of it shattered me. I tried to hide it from him, but he knew how I felt and did his best to console me . . .

* * *

"We're so lucky, we're truly blessed," he said one night in the garden, as he watered Jenna's pathetic little rose bush.

"Why do you bother with that silly thing?" she asked. "You can see it's dead, or pretty close to it."

Now, not so fast," he said. "This little bush might look droopy, but I have a hunch its got a lot of life inside it yet. Maybe it's just waiting for the right time to start blooming."

She grinned. "What an optimist."

"Sure." He grinned back. "But optimism brought me you, didn't it, pretty girl? And that's what I meant when I said we're lucky."

Lucky? She shivered in spite of herself. "You'll be leaving me soon— "

"Ah, darling, I'll never leave you," he said. And putting down the watering can, he gathered her in his arms and ran his lips down her cheek. "I love you," he whispered. "I love you body and soul, and we're going to get married, remember? just as soon as this bloody war is over."

"I wish we could get married now, today, right this minute."

"So do I! Oh, so do I, precious! I'd like nothing better than to make you my wife, but the army won't allow it in the work I'm in. They made me sign a paper when I joined this branch, stating no encumbrances—well, never mind that. The war won't last forever, and you've promised to wait for me. Remember?"

"Forever."

"That's my girl," he said, his lips warm and sweet on hers.

"So I was promised to him," she told Phoebe now, "and, as I said, the trouble was I never knew what happened to him."

"But you think the SS got him?"

Weezy shrugged. "I don't know. All I knew at the time was that he was leaving, my heart was breaking, and I had a kind of intuition—" She trembled, and tears filled her eyes. "I was desperately afraid that something awful was going to happen to him. He told me not to worry. He assured me he'd come back. And then, trying to cheer me up, he said that he wanted our last night to be one to remember.

"Let's go someplace really elegant, so when we're apart, we can hold the memory close, and we won't be so lonely. Is there any place special you'd like to go to, honey?"

"As a matter of fact there is," she said, wiping her eyes, determined to be brave for his sake. "Ever since I've been in New York, I've dreamed of going to the Plaza to hear Hildegarde." She hesitated. "But I'm afraid a night like that would be awfully expensive."

"So what?" Mickey said grandly. "If you want Hildegarde, we'll have Miss Hildegarde and a champagne supper besides." He said he'd make a reservation at the Plaza for the following Saturday.

But two days later when she got home from Julliard, she found a note from Mickey at her front door, asking her to meet him in Washington Square. She put the note in her purse, and as she was going out the door, she happened to glance in the garden and couldn't believe her eyes. And no wonder, for Jenna's pathetic-looking little rose bush seemed to have been mysteriously infused with life. Instead of drooping as it had been doing since it was put in the ground, it had straightened up, its leaves a sprightly green, and in its center bloomed one lovely white rose. She could smell the rose's fragrance even from the doorway where she stood. It was the most beautiful rose she'd ever seen, each petal perfectly shaped and glistening with dew. On impulse she got a pair of scissors from the drawer and clipped its stem. Then she walked to Washington Square.

She was a few minutes early, so as she walked around holding the rose, she noticed the square was filled with soldiers and sailors on leave. A lot of young mothers were there, too, pushing baby carriages, and old men playing chess on the benches. A group of teenage boys was bouncing a ball against the arch and shouting in high, excited voices. But where was Mickey?

She seemed to wait a long time and then when she was wondering if she'd read the note wrong, he came hurrying toward her. His shoulders were hunched in an odd way, like he was hurting inside, and his face was more somber than she'd ever seen it. She started toward him, arms outstretched. They met in the middle of the square and stood for several minutes, clinging to each other. Then he took her to a bench that two of the old chess players had just vacated.

"Thank God you're here," he said. "I just got my orders. Rudy and I will be leaving for overseas in about twenty-five minutes."

"You're catching a ship in twenty-five minutes?" She was incredulous.

"Not a ship. We're flying. But it's okay. I'm assigned to London for the time being. " He suddenly noticed the rose she was clutching in her hand. "Where'd you get that pretty thing?"

"It's for you," she said, handing it to him. "You were right about that poor little rose bush. It got a new spurt of life, and this beautiful rose is the result. Something, huh?"

"Told you," he said. "Why, this rose is really dazzling. I swear it's the prettiest I've ever seen." Laughing he lifted his hand and stuck the rose in his label, where it looked jaunty and bright against his olive drab uniform. "Thank you, sweetheart," he said. "I've got something for you, too." Reaching in his pocket he took out a piece of paper and handed it to her.

"What is it?"

"My APO number. You can write me there, and I'll write back. But don't worry if a spell goes by and you don't hear anything."

A spell? What does that mean? I can't stand it. I can't!

"I've given Rudy your address, just in case. He's promised to do his best to keep you informed, let you know what's going on if I can't write for a while."

A while? Oh, my God! she thought. She was dimly aware that he was speaking again, saying how rotten he felt that he couldn't take her to the Plaza on Saturday as he'd promised. "And after all my big talk, too," he said wryly, running a hand across his face. "But there just isn't time, I'm afraid. There's hardly time for anything, except a fast cup of coffee, maybe."

"Coffee's fine with me," she said, blinking back the tears.

So they found a little hamburger joint called the White Towers and ordered doughnuts and coffee, although Weezy couldn't eat the doughnut; it kept sticking in her throat. The place was crowded, but they finally managed to squeeze into a little corner table that offered some degree of privacy. Then suddenly a weatherbeaten old woman came in, and without so much as a by-your-leave, plunked herself down in the seat right across from them. She had a huge, ratty-looking purse and rheumy eyes, and when her coffee came, she opened her purse, and took out a flask, and poured a hefty shot of whiskey into her cup. Then she offered the flask to Mickey.

"Care for a little nip, soldier? Go on," she said hospitably. "You and the young lady there, both of you look like you could use a little cheering up."

"No, thanks," Mickey said in that nice way he had with everyone. "You're mighty kind, ma'am, but it would take more than a nip to cheer us up, I'm afraid."

"Oh?" She leaned closer. "What seems to be the trouble? You can tell me. I'm good at keeping secrets."

"Well, we're sad," Mickey told her, "because we're going to miss seeing Hildegarde. We were going to the Plaza Hotel to hear the world-renowned chanteuse Hildegarde sing, and we've been really looking forward to it—only something came up and now we can't go. It's a real disappointment."

"Tough," the old woman said. Then she smiled, showing all her gums, minus a couple of teeth, and added warmly, "But you're in luck, soldier. I'm a famous chantoosy myself. Actually, I don't mean to brag, but I'm much better known than this Hildegarde person." She winked. "In certain circles, that is."

"Is that a fact?" Mickey said, returning her smile. "What's your name, ma'am, if I may be so bold?"

"Marlene Dietrich," she told him. "That name ring a bell? Well, now you're looking at her, soldier. What would you like me to sing? Just name it—I know lots of tunes."

"What about *Lili Marlene*?" Mickey suggested. "Do you know *Lili Marlene* by any chance?"

"Do I know it? Why, dearie, I introduced that little ditty in the States." She took another nip from the flask, then throwing back her head, began singing in a high, cracked voice:

> *Underneath the lantern by the barrack gate,*
> *Darling I remember the way you used to wait.*
> *'Twas there that you whispered tenderly*
> *That you loved me, You'd always be*
> *My Lili of the lamplight, my own Lili Marlene.*

"That was delightful," Mickey said, when she had finished. Then the two of them sang a rousing duet of *The White Cliffs of Dover*, and everyone at the counter joined in when they got to *Over the Rainbow*.

By then everyone in the place, complete strangers, were laughing and enjoying themselves mightily, although Weezy couldn't help wishing she and Mickey could have a little time to themselves, in these last moments. But it was not to be. Suddenly Mickey looked at his

121

watch and jumping to his feet said he had to go, pronto! With that he took Weezy in his arms and kissed her, right in front of everyone. Then he kissed the old woman on the cheek and thanked her for giving them such a good time. And then he kissed Weezy again, a long, lingering kiss to last them the rest of their lives, and everyone in the place, all the people at the counter, applauded and wished him well. . . .

"So when he walked out the door, with the rose in his label," Weezy told Phoebe, "he was grinning like he was ready for anything. It was truly inspiring, just a marvelous sight."

There was a moment of silence, then Phoebe said, "But you never got to the Plaza to hear that Hildegarde person? What a gyp!"

"Oh, well." Weezy shrugged. "It was a disappointment, sure, but those things happen in wartime. You can't plan on anything, and it didn't really matter. I've never forgotten the White Towers, that funny little hamburger joint. What happened there left such an indelible impression on my mind."

Phoebe smiled. "You're cool, you're really cool, you know that, Weezy? But tell me, did Mickey write?"

"Oh, yes." Weezy dropped her eyes. "I got several beautiful letters from him, after he got to London. And he sent me my sweet little unicorn pillbox, which he said he found in a shop in Piccadilly Circus. But—" she sighed "—I never saw him again."

"How sad," Phoebe said, and impulsively she put her arms around her aunt and hugged her. "And you never knew for sure what happened to him?"

Weezy shook her head. "That's what haunts me. Rudy told me what he could, but it didn't help much. They were members of the OSS, the Office of Strategic Services, a US intelligence organization during World War Two. They'd parachuted into France after D-Day, about fifty kilometers north of Montpellier. Their assigned task was training partisans to infiltrate enemy positions. But Mickey, because of his German connections and his fluency in the language, had another assignment. His mission was to contact his cousin Otto if possible, who the Allies had learned was secretly working in the underground and help bring about Hitler's assassination. The Allies were all in on the plan which had been in the works for months, and Mickey's job was to coordinate the effort. This was an extremely dangerous mission for Mickey, obviously, because he had to go behind enemy lines and somehow rendezvous with Otto. But Rudy said Mickey was confident he could bring it off, and hopefully, if successful, it might shorten the war. So one night, without saying anything about it, Mickey slipped from his encampment, and no one ever saw him again. He was officially listed as Killed in Action."

"Do you think he ever found Otto?"

"It's possible—unless his uncle Bertram found him first. That's what I was afraid of. You see Bertram and Colonel Schatgstaff—"

"Were one and the same?" Phoebe guessed.

"Yes." Weezy nodded. "And I know what happened to Bertram. He was convicted in the Nuremberg trials after the war and hanged by the Allies for atrocities."

"Good riddance!" Phoebe said shuddering. "And Otto?"

She had been almost afraid to ask. But Weezy sighed and said sadly, "Otto was shot in the last days of the war when the Nazis discovered his plot to overthrow Hitler. Apparently there were several people in on the plot, which was just one of many to get rid of the monster, and I guess the Nazis disposed of the bodies of the so-called collaborators pretty quickly. At any rate, Rudy said the Allies could never discover if there was a lone American among the plotters."

"But you're hoping if Mickey had to die, it was with Otto?"

"Of course," Weezy said. "Perhaps it's foolish of me. I know it is after all this time, but it's haunted me for years. If only I knew Mickey didn't suffer." Biting her lip she looked away. Then getting ahold of herself, she added briskly, "But enough of that. After all this is our last night in Denver, and let's make it special."

"I'm all for that," Phoebe said, thinking how brave her aunt was.

They finished dressing a short time later, inserted their keycard in the door, and left to meet the others.

Chapter Sixteen

Franny had gotten someone to watch the baby, Buck took the evening off, and Weezy treated them all to dinner at the Brown Palace Hotel. They had a festive time with lots of laughter and reminiscing, and somewhere between dessert and coffee, Franny, who looked spectacular in one of her trousseau dresses of white silk, subtly motioned to Phoebe to leave the table. Puzzled, Phoebe followed her sister to the ladies room, where Franny showed her a personal check from Weezy for thirty thousand dollars made out to Franny and Buck.

"Wow!" Weezy said, eyes popping. "Looks like someone loves you!"

"Can you beat it?" Franny said. "She slipped it into my purse over the shrimp cocktail and whispered if I said anything, even one single word, she'd take it right back."

"Then keep your mouth shut," Phoebe advised. "I know that's going to be kind of difficult, knowing you, but you'll make a real effort. Right?"

"Silly." Franny laughed. "Of course we can't accept it."

"Sure you can. Weezy wants you to have it so Buck can open his restaurant."

"Well, it's the most generous, incredible thing I've ever heard of. But—" Franny frowned, "—so much money! Can she afford it?"

"She can. Believe me."

"Are you sure?"

"Positive."

"Well, I'm overwhelmed. This means all our dreams can come true. You know we were going to call the restaurant, if we ever got one, El Rancho, but now I think we ought to name it Chez Weezy. Whatta you think?"

"Hmm-mm, not bad," Phoebe said. "I like it. It has panache."

When they went back to the table, she saw Franny squeezing their aunt's hand. "Oh, Weezy—" she began.

Weezy cut her off. "Not a word," she warned, smiling. Turning to Jenna then, who seemed to have gotten over her tiff at being on the receiving end of her younger sister's largess, Weezy steered the conversation around to happy family memories. They all had a wonderful time and after dinner and a quick stop at the house for a final peek at the baby, Phoebe and Weezy returned to the motel. They went up to their room, put the key-card in the door and went inside. That's when they saw it—a long-stemmed white rose in the center of Weezy's pillow!

"Oh, my God!" Phoebe said. "Where'd that come from?"

"I have no idea," Weezy whispered. "But isn't it lovely?" She picked up the rose and held it close against her face, savoring its fragrance. "Didn't I lock the door when we left this evening?"

"Yes." Phoebe nodded. "I'm sure you did. I distinctly remember your putting the key-card in the door, and the maids don't work at night—so how did it get here?"

"Who knows?" Weezy said. "It's a mystery, no doubt about that."

But a mystery she didn't seem in any particular hurry to solve, Phoebe noticed. Indeed Phoebe thought her aunt was reveling in the strangeness of it all, as in the last few minutes, since she'd picked up the rose, her face had undergone a subtle transformation. Her features were more animated and her smile was the very picture of bliss. Her mood, too, seemed buoyant as she waltzed around the room, clutching the rose and looking completely happy, alive.

"Do you think—could it be a sign of something?" Phoebe asked, almost afraid to voice the strange thoughts that were swirling in her head. But then Weezy set her straight and removed all her fears.

"I think it's a gift," she said simply. "A beautiful gift that puts my heart to rest, and one we shouldn't question, not even for a moment."

"Amen," Phoebe said. And looking at her aunt, her sweet face shining with a newfound serenity, she suddenly thought to herself, *Hey, Mickey, thanks for coming through, guy.*

The next morning they packed and started the long drive back to New Mexico, the precious rose in a glass of water, resting in the cupholder between them. They had decided over breakfast to drive straight through on the return trip, and Phoebe figured they'd be in Santa Fe by four-thirty, five at the latest. They were making excellent time, and Weezy seemed to be in fine spirits, her face relaxed and wreathed in smiles.

"Oh, I'm so glad I saw them all, Jenna and Franny and the baby," she said. "And it wouldn't have been possible if you hadn't come along to help me drive, Phoebe dear. I'll be eternally grateful. I just can't thank you enough."

Phoebe was embarrassed. "Why, I should be thanking you," she said. "I had a good time," she added, after a moment, which was more or less true, even if things hadn't turned out like she'd hoped with Cody. When she thought back to their time together, it all seemed like a dream—the laughter and the moments of joy they'd shared. Her sense of loss was still so raw, it hurt to think of him. Yet strangely, she wasn't sorry for anything. Meeting him had been a phenomenon, an experience she'd never forget—and she still thought she'd apply for admittance to the University of Colorado as soon as possible.

She knew now she could still have a good life, albeit not exactly the one she'd dreamed of once. Weezy had taught her that. Her aunt had shown her, by her example, that one could cope, go on, in the face of terrible tragedy, tragedy much worse than anything she, Phoebe, had ever experienced. Weezy was so brave, she thought, so courageous.

"You know what?" she said suddenly. "You're a stalwart woman, Weezy. I don't think I ever met one before."

"A stalwart woman, am I?" That seemed to amuse Weezy. "Whew! I feel with a title like that, I should be leading a trek across the Rockies in a covered wagon."

"You could have done that, no sweat. For my money you're one gutsy lady."

"Why, thank you, darling. You're very sweet. But I'm afraid—" she sounded worried of a sudden, "—this isn't a very gutsy car."

"What's wrong with it?" Phoebe asked. She had noticed the car bucking when they passed through Fairplay, but hadn't thought much about it because Weezy didn't seem concerned.

"I don't know." Weezy frowned. "The darn thing keeps stalling for some reason. It stops, then it starts again, but in a few minutes— look, it's doing it now."

Sure enough, the car slowed and came to a stop on the crest of a hill. Weezy got it going again after a few tries. Plainly worried, she said, "I don't think we ought to be driving over the mountains in a car that sputters out for no reason. We'd better stop and have it looked at."

"Where?" Phoebe asked, glancing at the empty spaces all around them.

"I think the next town is Buena Vista," Weezy told her. "It should be right over the rise. They'll have a garage there. I just hope we can make it that far. Close your eyes and say a prayer."

"Okay." Phoebe dutifully closed her eyes and asked the Lord to help them. When she opened her eyes again not long afterwards, Weezy was pulling into a gas station on the outskirts of Buena Vista.

The man who came out to help them, a friendly Western type, heard their story and said it could be dirt in the gas, or a stuck float in the carburetor.

"Is that serious?" Weezy asked.

"Not very." He scratched his head. "But I won't know until I open the hood and look inside. I can't do that right now. My boy's gone to Fairplay and won't be back for half hour or so, and I'm all alone here. I'll try to crowd it in just as soon as I can, but it might be a while. I'd suggest you ladies find something to do instead of hanging around here."

What? Phoebe thought, as from the corner of her eye she saw a pickup pulling into the station. The truck was dusty and had definitely seen better days. Then she saw the driver, and her heart gave such a lurch, it almost stopped beating. It was soon obvious that Weezy had seen the driver too.

"Oh, Phoebe, look who's here," she said, sounding delighted. "Now that's what I'd call perfect timing." Impulsively she walked over to the pickup just as the driver opened the door. "Hello there, Cody," she said.

"Why, howdy, ma'am. Hello, Phoebe." His face lit up when he saw Phoebe, then he quickly dropped his eyes. A flush stained his cheeks.

"Hi," Phoebe said. She felt awkward, flustered, numb. And she didn't know where to put her eyes. "How come you're not working?"

"It's Monday, day off." As he talked he was unscrewing his gas cap and then filling the tank. Anything to avoid looking at her, she decided. "I thought you folks went to Denver."

"Oh, we did," Weezy said. "Had a wonderful time, too, and now we're on our way back to Santa Fe. But we're having trouble with the car. That nice man—" she gestured at the garage proprietor, "—is going to do his best to fix it, but he can't get to it for a while. So-o, it just occurred to me, now that we've run into one another, why don't we all have lunch? It's about that time. Will you join us, Cody? My treat."

"Weezy!" Phoebe protested, her face flaming. "I'm sure Cody has other plans for his day off."

He surprised her by saying, "Well, not really. As a matter of fact—" she noticed a muscle quivering in his jaw, "—I was just on my way to the Roundup to grab a sandwich. But we could go someplace else, if you'd rather."

"Why, the Roundup sounds just fine," Weezy said with a smile. "We'll ride with you, if you don't mind. Come along, Phoebe, hop in the middle."

She did as she was told, not having much choice, and the next thing she knew Cody had paid for his gas and helped Weezy into the truck, and they were barreling down the highway. She held herself stiffly upright, determined not to touch him, and sat so far over in the seat she was practically pushing poor Weezy out the door. Remembering her last time with Cody and the mess she'd made of things, her blood pounded and she was filled with pain and humiliation. She was also slightly miffed at her aunt for putting her in this situation—not that Weezy knew the whole story. . . or did she? Phoebe had told her very little about her breakup with Cody. It was simply too painful to discuss, but Weezy seemed to have an uncanny knack for figuring out things without being told. It was almost scary.

"Well, here we are," Cody said, a few minutes later, pulling to a stop. "This here's the Roundup, ma'am," he informed Weezy. "Hope you're not disappointed."

"I'm sure I won't be," Weezy said, as he helped her out of the pickup and they went inside. "This looks like a very interesting place. And you must be Wynonna," she added, smiling at the girl who came out of the room in back.

"You've got it," Wynonna said. Then she threw down a couple of menus on the nearest table and added in her quick, edgy voice, "So what can I get for you folks?"

"What would you recommend?" Weezy asked, as Cody held out a chair for her. She sat down and opened a menu.

"Well the chili dogs ain't bad," Wynonna told her. Turning to Phoebe she added pointedly, "Hey, I never thought I'd see you again. I thought you'd left."

Before Phoebe could answer, Weezy explained what had happened with their car. "We were just so fortunate to run into Cody at the garage. And as soon as our little buggy is fixed, we'll

129

be on our merry way, God willing. By the way I'm Weezy Burton, Phoebe's great-aunt."

"Pleased to meetcha, I'm sure," Wynonna said, temporarily put off by the warmth of Weezy's smile. She took their orders, chili dogs and Cokes all around, and was back in a remarkably short time with their food and drinks on a tray. Since the bar wasn't busy she pulled up a chair.

"Mind if I join you?" she said, crowding in between Cody and Phoebe. "Me and my pal here —" she patted Cody's arm, "— always eat lunch together on his day off, huh, Bro?"

"Bro" didn't answer. But Weezy said, "What a nice idea. And these chili dogs are really delicious. Did you make them, Wynonna? You're a fine cook."

"Ah, shoot, I don't know about that." She was blushing, obviously not accustomed to praise. "I do my best."

"And your best is very good I'm sure. Wynonna—such a lovely name. Were you named after a relative, or did your mother just like the sound of it?"

"Neither." A wry grin dawned on the pinched face. "I picked it out myself. My real name is June. June Moon—ever hear anything so silly? I don't know what my mama was thinking of when she saddled me with that clunker. But along about junior high I got sick of being teased about my name all the time and changed it to Wynonna."

"Like the Judds?"

"Right-o." She seemed surprised. "You know the Judds?"

"Not personally. But I admire their talent. I read somewhere that Naomi and Wynonna aren't the Judds' real names, either. It seems Naomi picked her name from the Bible—her real name is Diana—and Wynonna was baptized Christina. She chose her new name from a rock tune. Something called *Route 66*, I believe."

"No kiddin'?"

"I believe so. Apparently the Judds thought Naomi and Wynonna were better names for country singers, and I daresay they were right. Do you have aspirations of going into the entertainment business yourself, Wynonna?"

"Me?" She blushed scarlet. "Heck, no! I can't do nothin' but cook and clean—and raise purty flowers. I got a green thumb, if I do say so myself."

"Well, that's a lot to be proud of. But I thought Phoebe said you were going to California, to Hollywood, maybe?"

"We are—just as soon as I can scrape up the dough. But we're not going for me, no indeedy. We're going— " she patted Cody's arm again, "—so little brother here can crash the movies. He's so macho, he won't have any trouble getting discovered, you think?"

"That's a possibility," Weezy said. Turning to Cody she asked, "Have you always wanted to be a movie star?"

The question seemed to catch him off guard. "No-o," he sputtered, "heck, no! Being any kind of actor's just about the farthest thing from my mind."

Wynonna laughed. "Oh, there you go, being modest again." Then leaning closer to Weezy she confided, woman to woman, "Poor boy, he don't know what he wants."

"Sure I do," Cody snapped, his face red. "I'm not stupid, Wynonna."

"Never said you was, pal."

"Just for the record, what *do* you want, Cody? " Weezy asked. taking another bite of her hot dog. "Hmm-mm, this is so-o good, really delicious."

Cody shrugged. "I'm not sure. I won a scholarship to Boulder—"

"So Phoebe tells me. You should be very proud."

"Thanks. I wouldn't mind taking that, if I had my druthers."

Wynonna snorted. "Listen to the asshole!" She sounded furious all of a sudden. "Cody Moon, you know we've been through all that scholarship thing, and we decided it was just a bunch of crap."

"*You* decided Wynonna. I didn't! Just like you always decide what's best for me."

"Well, somebody has to. I sure can't see you wasting your time in

131

some stupid old classroom for four lousy years. Not when you could be a big movie star raking in the dough, living in some absolutely fab mansion complete with an Olympic-size swimming pool." Her eyes sparkled. "And we'd have servants at our beck and call, ready to spring to attention the minute you snapped a little finger."

"Hmm-mm, that certainly sounds intriguing," Weezy murmured. "But I'm curious, Wynonna. What would you be doing with yourself while Cody was off making movies? Wouldn't you get a little bored, just hanging around the mansion?"

"Shoot, no. I'll be his manager. The kid needs someone to watch out for him, see he don't get cheated, you know? That's how I get my kicks, taking care of my little bro. That's how it's always been, huh, Cody?"

"Yes," Cody said, scowling. "But maybe it's time I grew up, stood on my own two feet for a change. I'm not your little brother any longer, Wynonna, I'm a man. And—maybe it's time you realized that."

"Huh?" Her mouth dropped open, and she stared at him. Then she was laughing again. "Aw, go on with you. I ain't got time to listen to such foolish yappin'."

"Then you'd better take time," Cody said, his jaw set. His brows were drawn together in concentration, and he was wearing an inscrutable expression. Suddenly he reached across his sister and took Phoebe's hand. "I'm not going to California, and I'm not going to become a movie star. Come September I'm enrolling in Boulder, in the School of Engineering."

"The hell you say!" Furious, Wynonna slapped his and Phoebe's hands apart. "Over my dead body! You don't mean that, sonny boy."

"I mean exactly that!" He paused and inhaled a deep breath. "This is Independence Day, Sis. I'm a free man, my own man."

At last! Phoebe thought. Her heart began to thump, and she was so thrilled she couldn't believe this was happening.

Wynonna looked stricken, devastated. Then her eyes blazed. "Is this the thanks I get for working my fingers to the bone to give you everything, you ungrateful pup? For never having any life of my own because of you?"

"You didn't need a life of your own," Cody told her. "You had mine, Wynonna. And now I want it back. What's wrong with that?"

"I'll tell you what's wrong, you selfish swine." Her face contorted with fury. "After Mama left I raised you; you couldn't have lived without me. You owe me—"

"I know what I owe you, and I'm grateful," Cody said. "I'll always be grateful, and someday I'll try my best to make it up to you. But now it's time we went our own ways, made our own decisions. I've got to stand on my own two feet. It doesn't change how much I love you, Wynonna. I'll always love you. You're my sister."

"Liar! You dirty liar!" she screamed. "You took one look at her—" she glared at Phoebe, "—and you forgot all about me."

"I haven't forgotten." His voice was curiously gentle. "I don't want to hurt you, Wynonna. But this is the way its got to be. Try to understand."

"Aw. go to hell!" she exploded. "Just go to hell, and take your snobbish girlfriend with you. I don't need you."

"That's right," Cody said. "You don't need me, and the sooner you realize that the better—"

"Shut up!" She was screaming again, putting both hands over her ears. "Just shut your mouth, you traitor." Bursting into tears she jumped up from the table and ran to Leroy, the bartender, who was washing glasses behind the bar and had watched this scene with growing consternation. He put his arms around her, and took her to the room in back.

"Oh, Cody," Phoebe whispered, shaken. She was trembling all over at what she'd just witnessed, but felt strangely elated, too. "I'm sorry it had to come to this. But that was such a brave thing you did, standing up to her like that. It took a lot of courage, and I'm proud of you. We're both proud of you. Right, Weezy?" She turned to her aunt for confirmation.

"I couldn't have done it without you," Cody said.

She knew he said something else, but she didn't hear him, for looking at Weezy drove everything else from her mind. Her aunt was shaking as if she had a chill, and she was saying something strange and unintelligible. Phoebe realized, with a stab of fear, that something was drastically wrong.

"What is it?" she asked frightened, taking Weezy's hand.

Weezy made a valiant effort to smile, but her mouth twisted, and she seemed to be having trouble breathing. Terrified, Phoebe turned to Cody. "What'll we do? Do something!"

"Hang on," he said, and he put out his arms just in time to catch Weezy before she fell off the chair.

Her eyes closed, she was making gurgling noises in her throat now, and her head was lolling .

"She's got a pulse," Cody said, feeling her neck. "It's not very strong, but it's there. Let's lay her down on the floor, then I'll call 911 and get an ambulance."

"Okay," Phoebe said. "But hurry!"

Between them they eased Weezy to the floor. Cody left to make the call and Phoebe sat down beside Weezy, and cradling Weezy's head in her lap wrapped her arms around her. She wondered how long it would take to get an ambulance. Would it arrive in time? Weezy looked awful! She had never seen a face so pale.

Suddenly Weezy opened her eyes and stared directly at her. "Phoebe?"

"What is it? I'm here."

"In my purse—" She made a feeble gesture with her hand.

"You want something in your purse? Your pills? Sure. Why didn't I think of that?"

She looked around and spied the purse on the floor near her, where it had fallen. Picking it up she found the pillbox inside. She pressed the catch, and the lid, with the little white unicorn, popped open, revealing various colored pills.

"Which ones do you want?" she asked. "How many?"

"No—no pills." Weezy shook her head. "Won't help now. Want you—to have it."

"You want me to have your pillbox? Why, Weezy, I can't take that."

"Yes, you can. Its been my dearest possession. All these years. Mickey sent it to me from London—like I told you. Long time ago. But—I don't need it any longer. So I want you to have it, Phoebe, dear."

"Thank you," Phoebe said. "I'll cherish it always—I mean just always! I wish I'd known Mickey. He sounds like such a super guy."

"That he was," Weezy said. Her eyes, soft and luminous, seemed to be gazing into some far-off place. "So bright, so alive! With those dancing green eyes and that shock of red hair—well, he just couldn't be missed."

Green eyes, red hair? Phoebe thought, startled. Little Shilo Dawn had big green eyes and a thatch of flaming red hair. No one in the family could figure out where she got her coloring. But, of course. It was so obvious! Mom was Weezy's daughter, not Jenna's daughter, as they'd always thought. Which meant Weezy was Phoebe's and Franny's grandmother. And therefore little Shilo Dawn, with her green eyes and red hair, was Weezy's—and Mickey's—great grandchild. How could she have been so blind?

Weezy was struggling to speak again. "I thought—he was truly beautiful. If a man can be beautiful."

"Mickey was, I bet," Phoebe said, her throat tightening. An immense sadness enveloped her for a moment, when she thought of all the lost years. Then she smiled down at her aunt and drawing her closer, started rocking her gently back and forth.

Cody came back a short time later and knelt beside them. "The ambulance will be here soon," he whispered, touching Phoebe's arm. "How's she doing?"

"It's too late." Tears streamed down Phoebe's face unchecked.

Cody took a closer look at Weezy. "Oh, honey girl, I'm sorry. Just so sorry, I can't tell you…. Don't cry."

"It's all right. I'm not crying because she's gone. I'm happy."

"You're happy?" he said, puzzled.

She nodded and leaned against his shoulder. "You know something, Cody? I think Weezy is just where she wants to be. At long last!"

The End